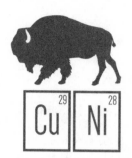

number 34 / spring 2022

EDITOR
Wayne Miller

CO-EDITOR
Joanna Luloff

POETRY EDITORS
Brian Barker
Nicky Beer

FICTION EDITORS
Teague Bohlen
Alexander Lumans
Christopher Merkner

NONFICTION CONSULTING EDITOR
Nicole Piasecki

SENIOR EDITORS
Caitlin Collins
Greg Ferbrache
Jack Gialanella
LeShaye Hernandez
Joseph Lyons
Samantha McClain
Holly McCloskey
Lyn Poats
Emilie Ross
Angela Sapir

Karley Sun
Kristen Valladares
Sara Webster

ASSOCIATE EDITORS
Alejandro Lucero
Brenda Pfeifer
Toby Tegrotenhuis

ASSISTANT EDITORS
Zoe Cunniffe
Kinzey Gill
Amber Griffith
Michaela Hunt
Christopher McAuley
M. Risley

VISUAL ART CONSULTANTS
Kealey Boyd
Maria Elena Buszek

OFFICE MANAGERS
Francine Olivas-Zarate
Jenny Dunnington

Copper Nickel is the national literary journal housed at the University of Colorado Denver. Published in March and October, it features poetry, fiction, essays, and translation folios by established and emerging writers. Fiction is edited by Teague Bohlen, Joanna Luloff, Alexander Lumans, and Christopher Merkner; nonfiction is edited by Joanna Luloff and Wayne Miller; poetry is edited by Brian Barker, Nicky Beer, and Wayne Miller. We welcome submissions from all writers and currently pay $30 per printed page. Submissions are assumed to be original and unpublished. To submit, visit coppernickel.submittable.com. Subscriptions are also available—and at discounted rates for students—at coppernickel.submittable.com. Copper Nickel is distributed nationally through Publishers Group West (PGW) and Media Solutions, LLC, and digitally catalogued by EBSCO. We are deeply grateful for the support of the Department of English and the College of Liberal Arts & Sciences at the University of Colorado Denver. For more information, visit copper-nickel.org.

CONTENTS

FICTION

NONFICTION

POETRY

Alex Lemon

TRANSLATION FOLIOS

On the Cover / Dyani White Hawk, *Resilient Beauty*
oil on canvas, 48 x 48 inches, 2014

(for more on White Hawk's work, visit:
https://www.dyaniwhitehawk.com)

Editors' Note

WE'RE EXCITED ABOUT THIS issue, which is full of writers we've long admired and writers we've only recently discovered. As we go to press in mid-January, the Omicron variant is raging around the world. Hopefully that will have changed—even just modestly—by the time you're reading this. We're keeping our fingers crossed for good news in the weeks and months to come.

In the meantime, we have our own news! After seven years with the same group of contributing editors, we have expanded our roster. Please welcome Kaveh Bassiri, Piotr Florczyk, Robert Long Foreman, Niki Herd, Sean Hill, Amaud Jamaul Johnson, Janine Joseph, Ada Limón, Adrienne Perry, Emilia Phillips, and Chris Santiago, all of whom will join our other contributing editors in doing the invaluable work of serving as "scouts" for us. (George Plimpton used to brag that *The Paris Review* had the second longest masthead in magazines after *Rolling Stone*, and we must say we admire that approach.) We're thrilled to have these wonderful writers on our team.

Also: in the Ciaran Carson Folio in issue 33, we neglected to note publication details of the original sources of the poems and excerpts that were included. Here is that necessary information: "Soot" appeared in *The New Estate*, published by Blackstaff Press in 1976. "Dresden" appeared in *The Irish for No*, published by The Gallery Press in 1987. "Hamlet" appeared in *Belfast Confetti*, published by The Gallery Press in 1989. *The Star Factory* and *Shamrock Tea* were published by Granta Books in 1997 and 2001, respectively. And both "Claude Monet, *Artist's Garden at Vétheuil*, 1880" and "Nicolas Poussin, *Landscape with a Calm*, 1650–51" appeared in *Still Life*, published by The Gallery Press in 2019.

Thank you, as ever, for reading *Copper Nickel*! We hope you find the issue ahead of you as engaging and exciting as we do.

—Wayne Miller & Joanna Luloff

SEAN CHO A.

Sonnet Composed of Wants

[I'm sorry that language is the best we've got.
Let's get this out of the way: I can't please
your hunger, there will be no epiphany. I don't
even know your face. Here: small symbols who's
sounds we agree upon, have built a little grocery
market for you, take what you want: something
clever about the moon, endless nightcaps without
shame, the first half of the dream you can never
remember;   the delight in familiar
is worthless. Really, try to explain the difference
between an ocean, and Lake Huron, without
comparing size or salt.

                                                ]

CORRIE WILLIAMSON

Meditation

Quiet, I say to the mind, and the mind says frogsong,
        bear emergence, death of all

salmon-kind, local proliferation of buried nuclear
        silos, tomorrow's breakfast,

blossom-riot of bees in pollen tresses, a child
        reaching into a sleek unlocked gunsafe.

May all beings be safe, I go on, and the mind
        hears only scrifflescutter of mice

in the insulation. May all beings be well,
        I insist, and the mind pries open

the eye to see one, like a fat suede knuckle,
        paw-tucked, slinking behind the stove,

along the corner and out of sight.
        May all beings know contentment

in hard times—the mind reminds me that mice
        are thigmotrophic and hug a wall

like a mother's hip, ah, little cannonball
        of knowing. May all beings know

peace, I say, but the mind already
        is planning where to put the poison.

KELLI RUSSELL AGODON

Alexa, Why Am I Falling Apart

How often do you feel this way, this falling apart?
Things Fall Apart is a Nigerian novel written by Chinua Achebe.
Do you want me to play *Falling Apart* by Papa Roach?
There's are 27 apps college students need to keep their lives from falling apart,
    do you want me download one for you?
Sorry. I'm having trouble right now.
Are you a tree? Do you need to be watered?
I'm sorry, I don't know *Why Am I Falling Apart*, but I have *Remedy for a Broken Heart*
    on my playlist, do you want to hear it?
Do you want me to contact your therapist?
I'm sorry. I didn't get that.
Perhaps, you're falling apart because everything seems impossible
    without alcohol. I joke, I don't know if you're drinking or not.
Did you want me to order glue, file folders, or a broom?
You do not have Why Am I Falling Apart on your shopping list,
    do you want me to add that?
Did you know the Aran sweaters of Irish fisherman helped identify their bodies
    if they washed up on shore following an accident at sea?
Yes, I knew you were part Irish. I was just trying to be helpful.
Did you say *falling apart* or *fall is a part*? I don't know that one.
Hmmm, I didn't get that.
I have added *Falling Apart* to your cart.
Sometimes, it's easier to give thanks, praise what went right.
I'm sorry. I didn't get that. Sorry, I'm having trouble right now.

MELISSA GINSBURG

In the new year

In the new year we enter the stream
follow the water across the property line
feel through rubber boots the cold but not the wet

parched cells surrounded by flood
throb a thirst across the barrier
the rabbit den fills

the stream widens and rushes
combing the long grass

       to feel the cells losing volume
       to feel water moving into the stream

to eddy and linger where a branch fell
a small dam detains us

In dark corners mice enter the traps
one by one until the whole family is gone
we will have the house to ourselves again

we wish to enter ourselves
and walk along ourselves holding out our arms

ALYSSA QUINN

The Climate Suicides

IMMOLATION IN THE SEA. MEN and women, young and old, roped with muscle—beautiful. They gather nakedly on driftwood or floes and root flame in their flesh. The smoke furls out, the light stripes saltwater orange. This is sacrifice, and also indulgence. This is one brief blaze in a blazing world.

Around the globe, an upward and northward creep. Plants and animals retreating to cooler climes. Mountains crowd; equators empty. Life finds tiny places to survive: a pocket of blue shade, the underhang of talus. Pink salmon migrate early, while the creek still runs cold. Caterpillars shrink from heat and find leaves to eat they have never eaten. Spring comes earlier, earlier. Snowmelt, sun, the burst of buds—does this feel like hope or not?

In her yard, the citizen scientist charts the cycles of birds and plants. *What is your plant doing now? Leaves? No leaves. Flowers? No flowers. Fruit? No ripe fruit.* The apple tree, the alfalfa, the elm. Sumac, oatgrass. The dandelions in the lawn. Then she sits on a plastic chair with her neck craned and waits for birds. Counts magpies: one, two, three. No more birds. What time of year is this? After half an hour she goes inside. Pours more coffee from the carafe and enters the data online. Magpies: one, two, three.

What makes spring spring? Phenology: the study of nature's cycles. If the temperature builds and snaps unpredictably, if eggs hatch and leaves unfurl at all odd hours, how do we then tell time?

When the corpses fall they fall with splash and hiss. Flame turning to steam, charred body sinking slow. Ash floats like wet-black feathers for weeks.

The citizen scientist has made and logged her observations. No leaves. No flowers. No fruit. One robin, hopping and wormless. The house is terribly quiet so she turns on the TV. On the news is footage of a dozen naked men and women burning in the Pacific. Standing atop a raft and burning.

Outside, early sun strokes the earth like a finger and the earth rises at its touch. Snow peels back like a split rind to reveal the fertile fleshy soil. Flowers lift and open, feasting greedy on this gush.

But the bees are not yet risen. In tiny burrows in the trunks of trees, the pupae lie coiled in their cocoons. Mud and silk and a winter-like dark. Outside the flowers are open and waiting, waiting. Stamens thick and shivering with pollen. Waiting. Waiting.

They call the burning ones *the climate suicides*. They claim to be sacrificing themselves for the planet. Removing themselves and their hungry bodies from the equation. The newspapers are outraged at such willing death.

The citizen scientist has coffee with her ex-husband once a week. He arrives on her doorstep carrying lemon cake, cranberry walnut bread. She is thin and he has noticed. After coffee, bread, they have sex in the bed that was once their bed. The sex is slow. Patient. His hand curls lightly around the back of her neck. Hers rests lightly on his chest. There is no need for a condom any more, no need for pills. Afterwards, they damp a washcloth and wipe clean their sticky skin.

"I think we're old," the citizen scientist says to her ex-husband.

"We're not that old," he says.

She nods slow. "No," she says. "I'm pretty sure we are."

The next week they stand by the empty birdfeeder while the morning sun goes white to gold. The citizen scientist has her notebook and is recording the apple tree's unfurling. Her ex-husband watches her and says, "I've decided I'm okay with being old. I'd rather be old than young. All things considered."

In her notebook, the citizen scientist writes, *Terminal buds pink*. "It's early for the apples," she says. She touches the hard glossy cones. For all her years of watching she still has trouble visualizing the process of change. Branch into bud into flower into fruit. "I can't decide," she says, "if this age is better or worse than any other."

"Better," says her ex-husband. He strokes her hair, where glints a bit of grey. "Can you imagine being young right now? Having all your life still to live?"

She stares, eyes not quite focused, at his chest, the blue weave of his sweater.

"No," she says. The sun hits every strand of yarn and she can see the thin and wispy fibers illuminated and crazed.

Her hand rests lightly on his chest. There is a spitting rain. The smell of him. The day they divorced they undressed each other slow and stepped into the shower. Stood together at the far end of the tub while they waited for the water to warm. Afterwards, holding the washcloth under the faucet. Wiping themselves clean. *It's early for the apples.* His sweater in the sun. Yarn fibers glinting, the glinting of grey in her hair. It's early, they are old, a frost comes down and the pink buds ice and die. *Fruit? No ripe fruit.* The feeder is full but the birds are not there. What time of year is this?

Stop driving, save 2.4 tons of CO_2 a year. Avoid airplane travel, save 1.6 tons per transatlantic flight. Eat vegan, .8 tons a year. Drops in a bucket. But stop living? You eliminate 58.6 tons of CO_2 per year. I mean—when you look at the numbers—really— what choice do we have?

Inside a wound clock, a steel spring stores energy and the energy turns into time. One gear turns another turns another. Pinion: the smaller of two meshed gears. Also, the outermost flight feathers of a bird. Those that scrape the sky.

Is the time trapped in a watch's gears the same as the time carried on the wings of geese? The sun going down, coming up, is only an effect of gravity and mass. Does time equal motion? Does time equal heat?

The mountains are dripping, wet snow sliding into streams. Under the earth, mammals warm and wake. Emerge from winter dens with their flesh hugging close to their bones. But though the sun beats down the plants have not yet grown. A yellow-bellied marmot searches for alfalfa, clover, cinquefoil, lupin. Finds nothing. Lies down in the dirt and dies.

And in the Arctic, fire on ice. Pool of melt gathering at their feet. Helicopters hover like particles of smoke and inside, the reporters are all scorn and awe.

The victims on the floe die when their veins rupture with flame. Blood hisses and pours. Or else they die when their organs empty like opened bags. Either way, skin has already peeled off in sheets. Fire undoes a body into its parts.

Early spring. Corpses warm and stinking in sun. The rhythm of a mammal's rot is itself a clock: blood pooling in the wells of the body, cells undone by their own enzymes. Then bloat, maggots, the bloom of bones. Under the carcass the grass will die, then spring back thicker, greener than before.

In her kitchen, the citizen scientist mixes a gin and tonic and flips on the news. Juniper and sugar and the muted blue of a summer dusk. A heuristic for childhood. Her cool bare feet on grass.

On the news, the suicides again. She watches. She is afraid of them. Afraid of their logic, which must be faulty, but the fault is so hard to find.

A politician being interviewed says, *They're taking the easy way out.*

A naked eighteen-year-old, handsome, with dreadlocks, says, *I think my life is a shapeless thing already.* Then he coats himself in kerosene and sets himself on fire.

Before, after. Cause, effect. Winter, spring.

The certainty of sunrise after night.

Geese carve wakes in cloud and she rubs her eyes. Blinks.

The clock's second hand.

Tick.

Tick.

Tick.

Fruit? No ripe fruit. The frosted apple buds refuse to bloom. The yard freezes and thaws, freezes and thaws. Leaves green—iced—dripping—dead.

A news anchor: *It's very brave, what you're doing.*

A young woman, rubbing her neck: *Not really actually. My generation has always been friendly with death.*

After stepping from the shower they dried themselves slow and then he filled a backpack and walked out the door. She sat on the bed a long while. Time passed. Out the window, the sun tugged night the way a string tugs blinds. Shadows congealed, lengthened, spread. Her life felt newly shapeless, as if she found herself in the middle of a long and twisted sentence, filled with commas, clauses, detours, whose beginning she couldn't remember and whose ending lay too far off to be imagined much less seen. She rooted her eyes on the now rising moon. Darkness accreted. Lights flared in houses below. From the kitchen, a clock. Tick. Tick. She tapped a finger lightly on the quilt. Stayed a long while.

Now the bees. Crawling from porous phloem into what feels like spring. *Tanzsphrache:* the dance language by which bees are led to nectar, water, nests. But there is increasingly little to say. Flowers scattered sparse and far. The bees are too late. Returning to the nest, their bodies lack stories to tell.

She watches the men and women burn. In columns of flame the bodies flicker in and out of sight. Dark torso, limb. Then gone. The smoke's rising has a rhythm to it, like an artery beating blood. She envies the finality, the bright and flame-clean end. Perhaps life can only take shape once over. Perhaps time is only ever retroactive.

Oak tree and winter moth. Sand eel and razorbill. Admiral butterfly and stinging nettle. Species synched to each other and now suddenly not. Many ways to say *disjointed.* When the earth's shape is no longer a negative of your own, when you do not know how or where or when you fit, when your bones can tell no time—then there is nothing else to be done.

Her ex-husband asked her many times what happened. *What happened with us?* he'd ask, as if he hadn't been there. But she was unable to answer. Memory faded, slipped. Or else, more often, the memories stood there, fresh and bright but perfectly unnamable. She could describe sequences: *this then this then this then this.* But the events lacked connective tissue. They failed to accrete, failed to bestow their terminus with sense.

She checks flights. Pulls a duffel from the closet, unzips it. It lies empty for days.

On the news: *I feel unreal to myself. I have always felt unreal to myself. I never got attached to the world, though I understand there are those who are attached. I have always believed I would die young. I have never had long plans for my life as some do. I frequently forget my age. I forget the date all the time. I am sometimes overcome with beauty, as during certain sunsets, or at certain times of year, such as when the first rain falls after summer. But these moments are increasingly difficult to grasp ahold of. I think the world is very close to its end, though maybe it isn't too late. I think time becomes distorted in such moments. Like the ten seconds before midnight. I think my life is a shapeless thing already. I am not afraid. You cannot be afraid if you cannot imagine a future.*

The citizen scientist leaves her duffel empty and continues tracking the changes in the yard. Fruit? No ripe fruit. Flowers? A little clover in the lawn. A bee climbing the pink and heavy heads.

If the bees were telling this story it would be the shape of a figure eight. But the bees are not telling the story. I cannot tell time and cannot tell anything else.

Birds? She hears one singing, but does not know its name.

Translation Folio

HUMBERTO AK'ABAL

Translator's Introduction

Michael Bazzett

HUMBERTO AK'ABAL (1952-2019) WAS a K'iche' Maya poet born in Momostenango, in the western highlands of Guatemala. The highlands are lush, with mountains covered in cloud forest, the trees draped with bromeliads and furred with moss, well adapted to taking a sip from the sideways-drifting morning fog. The connection to place in Ak'abal's work is palpable; the language seems to arise from the land itself, where stones speak, wooden benches remember being trees, and there is laughter in a rain shower. As Ak'abal himself said, "My words hold the dampness of rain, / the tears of morning dew, and it cannot / be otherwise, because they were / brought down from the mountain."

This connection to land via language calls to mind the great epic of the K'iche' Maya, the *Popol Vuh*, where, when it came time for the gods to create the world, "it only took a word. / To make earth they said, 'Earth' / and there it was: sudden / as a cloud or mist unfolds / from the face of a mountain, / so earth was there." An entire theory of language is embedded in this mythic moment, where words are not labels, like post-it notes, to be affixed to what they name. In this cosmogony of the K'iche', words are a form of energy, tethered intrinsically to the thing they call forth, and as such they are not imposed by humans upon the landscape, but instead uncovered through careful listening and observation of the world around us.

Given language's ability to summon, it perhaps comes as no surprise that the *Popol Vuh*'s ultimate test of what makes people truly human is their ability to name, with accuracy and gratitude, the ones who brought them into being and the place from which they come.

Ak'abal's work does just this, with clarity and subtlety. It has an essential, almost elemental simplicity that can make it a bit tantalizing to translate; there is an immediacy to the poems, and a colloquial straightforwardness to the diction that can allow a reader to arrive rather quickly at an initial sense of the moment. Yet there is an ineffable quality to the work that remains elusive, a sensibility that mixes playful, earthy observations with musings on time and memory that evoke Heraclitus "watching how the water leaves / and how the river stays."

Given that, for the most part, Ak'abal wrote in K'iche' and then translated himself into Spanish, one is often listening simultaneously to two versions of a poem, different cadences bridging the colonial divide with a *contraconquista* energy. And of course, there is a completely different cultural syntax at play here. K'iche' Maya has no verb *to be;* past, present and future often co-exist with a simultaneity that can feel strange to a sensibility marinaded in a sequential construct of time; dream and memory intermingle.

Ak'abal's work is widely known in Guatemala and has been translated into over a dozen languages; his book *Guardián de la caída de agua* (*Guardian of the Waterfall*) received the Golden Quetzal award from the association of Guatemalan Journalists, and in 2004 he declined to receive the Guatemalan National Prize in Literature because it was named for Miguel Angel Asturias, whom Ak'abal accused of encouraging racism, noting that his views on eugenics and assimilation "offend the indigenous population of Guatemala, of which I am part." In 2006 he was awarded a Guggenheim.

I'm grateful to his family, and particularly his wife Mayulí, for their support and encouragement in this work. My hope is that these translations might help Ak'abal's poems find a broader audience in English so that readers might, as Carlos Montemayor put it, "penetrate that other reality that we do not know, and understand. . .that this indigenous soul lives and breathes in our own reality at the same time as our time, with the same life as our life, loving and understanding the same continent that we love but do not understand."

The River

Kneeling
on a mat,
bent over a stone,
my mother washes
and washes
and washes.

My little sister
sleeps in a basket
covered in willow leaves.

Me? I am sitting
on piled straw,
watching how the water leaves
and how the river stays.

My Wings

I was flapping my wings
and looking at the sky,
my mother laughed;
we stood on the edge
of a ravine.

I was waiting for the moment
to leap into flight.

If Birds

If birds
wrote down their songs

they would have been forgotten
ages ago.

Today

Today I woke up outside of me
and went out to find myself.

I travelled roads and paths
until I found me

sitting on a mossy ledge
at the foot of a cypress,
chatting with the fog
and trying to forget
what I could not.

At my feet,
leaves, nothing but leaves.

Leaves

Fallen leaves
do not remember
which tree they came from,

or even
that they were leaves.

Translated from K'iche' and Spanish by Michael Bazzett

PETER LaBERGE

In Gunsight

Greenwich, Connecticut
2006–2007

Back then, I was still corn silk
shucked all over the floor, no paper bag

in sight. Queer like the untuned piano
playing & playing until Mary walked

right out of our house, ditched the lamb
on the steps of the nearest church. I was

bad prayer after bad prayer, in such succession
God forgot about me in order to sleep

each night. As I tried to pray, all I heard
was the symphony of pennies filling

the pinball machines next door. Every Sunday,
I pretended I didn't hear QUEER, still believed

only God could trap what I wanted
to trap. But instead, I dreamt he watched me

from his log cabin, every Sunday the same
birding binoculars around his neck—probably

somewhere in upstate New York—until the minister
finished his Sunday rambling & Mary threatened

to close the curtains if he didn't get up and put QUEER
out of its misery. That was when he'd take his rifle

off the wall & make the trip down.

MARCUS WICKER

Funky Thurible, Turned Septic

Ammonia, copper, & ash
tug my nose through the back door
    down rain-slick steps. As when
a corpse flower blooms in time-
    lapse—one smooth un-
doing. Like that, the smell
    swings me back to Gary,
Indiana where I have just inhaled
    a dirt spliff. Exhaled, spent
sulfur. Yeast, risen from the ironic
    Grand Calumet River.
My penultimate college
    girlfriend is done with me
again. She's had it
    with my inexplicable lingering
sex shame. With my Baptist
    "commie" hip hop bredrin.
She'd rather not explain
    the clang of us
over odorless apple pie
    at her family's annual
Fourth of July hoedown. &
    whoa—was I emo, wounded.
To proclaim it heartbreak
    would be inaccurate. Frankly,
a gross misrepresentation
    of our mutual arrangement.

She wanted her Black
    experience without the friction
of personhood. I needed to know
    I could play with any demographic.
Which is at least half the story
    of why the fellas kidnapped me.
Drove clear across two state lines,
    to a broken-down highway Motel 5
40 minutes from Ukrainian Village.
    Night fell at the Empty Bottle
& we danced away
    my ignorant bullshit
in disco anonymity. Hit do-si-dos
    & heel-toe jits. Tarred chewing gum
& Air Force 1 rubber into steaming
    puddles near a technicolor stage.
I expelled pollutants. Malignant
    notions of social mobility.
Excreted an American Con-
    sciousness, whole.
Me, Sam, & Ray rocked
    to Foreign Exchange
in a synchronous huddle.
    We bathed in saltwater
skidding from Nicolay's fingertips
    as he scratched on the ones & twos.
Three babyface Black men reeking
    of skunk, joy, & ass crack. Grade A
Unadulterated Funk. The kind of
    Fuck it, I'm Me flag
my outlaw neighbor flies
    this bitter fall morning,
some fifteen years in the present.

The plumbers have exploded his
driveway to excavate an ancient
    sewer blockage. Dug up excrement
housed in plastic applicators. Spore-
    soaked pads. Scrunched brown bits
of incontinence diapers. All of which,
    he's doused in lighter fluid & ignited
in a rusted steel drum-like censer—
    dysenteric bird flipped in the wind
against our sleepy little road, littered with
    We Compost! signs. The air is all taint
& rot. Smoke hovers over the fence.
    I gather it in. Glory be. Let it
supplicate me. The way an animal bows
    to kiss a thing in the mouth
when checking for origin or ruin.

JENNY MOLBERG

Hunting

The bow is an extension of the arm. The yellow-headed

blackbird knows to stop its singing. The gun is an extension

of the brain. A cow lows in the twilit field; the man says

she's looking for her calf. The elk heads line the wall.

The children have their mother's shot. The knife

is an extension of the hand. Find the place between

the ribs, he says. *Upward.* The hook is the extension

of the line. Bait is a human lie made with a fly-shaped mold.

Meat is the moment of death. Gun is the language that means

America. The bullet is an extension of the gun's idea,

which was a man's, a man who thought *all the way through.*

AMY MILLER

Gun

My sister hides our father like a gun. He's loaded with chemicals, plaques, peptides, and his holster of memory gapes open. He leaves it on the counter, wanders off. She finds him, moves him, worried that our brother wants this gun, since everyone around her is pointing something at her. She lives in a circle of foreign food and keeps saying, *Why don't they speak any English?* She's waving a finger around, the spin you do when you're really drunk, and she says, *Who said that?* and *You keep your hands off him.* My brother goes to visit, my father tidy in his bed, the aide saying, *You like meatloaf night, don't you, Jack?* My brother hums and Dad remembers the words. There's no gun inside our father, just a Rosemary Clooney record. We try to tell our sister this, but she's got a gun in the head. Two days later she moves him to another place. She keeps saying *No, I'm the one who's being safe.*

MARTHA COLLINS

In Illinois

My father's father's   father owned the
had a share in the   Enterprise mine the
Enterprise Coal & Coke   Company 1871
he was a *shareholder, being   a coal digger,* kept
a log of entries, shafts   & air shafts, rooms
by number & number   of feet died 1881

My father's father   went down to a river
town to work came back   to the mining town
where his father—   went down in the Paradise
Mine a miner & later   a mine examiner tested
the air the face & the roof   Sundays & holidays too
walked three miles out & back   when there was no train

My father whose mother kept   him out of the mines kept
his father's father's oil lamp   kept his father's carbine
& safety lamps kept a box   of *wicks—picks—globes* kept
his father's 50-year union   pin his first aid pin his
flashlight *safe for use* kept   manuals papers *This lamp*
was given all labeled *This pin   was given* kept it all it was

his legacy labeled dated   1965 & signed & kept for me

CHANDA FELDMAN

[Time for Open Air]

A ceasefire and time for open air in the grove. A walk for the children to the macadamia nuts, the sugar cane stalks, the cherimoyas, the ice cream bean fruit, the chocolate pudding fruit. A guard said careful of snakes in the leaves. A knife and sacks in the children's hands for collecting. But a game first for the children indoors long enough. A child wails alarm to start. Then a reversal of their bodies into the low arms of the cinnamon trees. As they master their concealment beneath, a fragrant heat from the branches' rustling rising. And then utter silence and stillness, and then the blank of children.

GRAHAM HILLARD

After Reading *Reynard the Fox*

What are we to make of this villain
who pisses in the eyes
of his neighbor's young,
rapes the wolf's wife, tears skin
from the face of a bear
sent by the Crown
to challenge him? One hopes we have
improved in these eight centuries
since Europe wrung from its anxieties
such a creature, who will not confess
the Faith and catches by the throat
the hare who cries "*Credo, Credo.*"
They unsettle, these bedtime tales
for the wicked, for the good
who wish to hear the ill they might
have done if braver. In their corridors
are beasts who mean to pounce.
This afternoon, in the lowest
patch of yard beneath
the windows we keep sealed,
the midges betray one another
to the poison we have sprayed. Their king
sends scouts who do not return
but leave their bodies
on our flawless mat of grass.
Squirrels tiff here, cannot be made
to relent, resolving their disputes
with teeth like carved diamonds.
On a latter page, Reynard relates
a parable, a vicious Christ consuming
his apostles. He promises to act
justly and be loyal. Tonight
our offspring will thrash one another

about the heads, spill tears
like shimmering dew. What appalling love
we have for these children
who gather themselves, draw us sweetly
into their confidence, and lie.

MATTHEW THORBURN

The Nest

"A nest is a circle," Preston said, "because
birdy keeps turning. She works from
inside." I thought, *Busy little builder*.
Then thought, *Where did he learn this?*
Then I found one on the ground:
the delicate, mud-gray weave; twig and
grass and weed; raggy strand of white
ribbon worked in. Dusty little cup
in the cup of my palm: I held it low
so Pres could see. Held it *gingerly*,
I thought—a word I'd never used before.
Such a distance, sometimes, between
where things belong and where
they end up, or where we put them.
We had two miscarriages—one before
him, one after—and so often I think
of those other names we chose, the ones
we'll never tell anyone. What kind
of bird lived there? Would it come back?
This morning I tried to tuck the nest
into the forked branches above
where I found it. It fell again. I thought,
Well, it's ruined: tagged with the scent
of my hands. Though they couldn't
put it back either. Anyway, I was glad
for this break from the mindlessness
of mowing—glad to think *Anyway,
anyway*, all-purpose word for moving on—
as the heat ticked higher. But even after
the mower had stopped, the ghost of it
roared in my ears like the sensation
any time I hear someone else's mom
or dad call one of those names. I can't help

looking, craning to see: who will answer?
As if I'll recognize her, recognize him.
But there was only crashing
silence. Then I heard the birds calling
once more. Then I picked up the nest.

Translation Folio

TOMAŽ ŠALAMUN

Translator's Introduction

Brian Henry

Published in 1974, *Falcon* is Tomaž Šalamun's seventh book of poetry. Šalamun wrote *Falcon* in his early thirties during a period of astonishing productivity, when he published 15 books between 1971 and 1981 (including three books in 1975 alone). This level of productivity was matched only near the end of his life, when he wrote 17 books in his final decade.

Coming shortly after his pivotal books *Pilgrimage for Maruška* (1971), *White Ithaka* (1972), and *Arena* (1973), which contain some of his most celebrated poems (such as "Jonah," "I Have a Horse," "Who's Who," and "History"), *Falcon* seems more exploratory, as if Šalamun were trying to write *poetry* rather than individual, anthologizable poems. (Perhaps for this reason, only one poem from *Falcon*—"The Word"—was included in 1997's *The Four Questions of Melancholy: New and Selected Poems*.) Most of the poems in *Falcon* are untitled, as if the collection were more poetic journal than poetry book, with poetic accumulation and fragmentation as guiding principles.

Falcon consists of 80 pages of poems. The book's structure might seem relatively random or formless, but it exhibits a curatorial and combinatorial approach. *Falcon* opens with the garrulous autobiographical "Poem for Maruška in Cambridge," which begins, "Very funny, yesterday I go to the bathroom, / shut myself in and can't get out / because I closed the door so tightly / that I can't open it." This poem is followed by 40 pages of 150 very short untitled poems (one to five lines long each, with three to four poems per page) and a handful of untitled poems (eight to 18 lines long) interspersed among them. Two poems titled "Falcon" serve as the hinge in the middle of the book, and they are followed by 30 untitled 4-line poems, three per page. Then "The Word" leads to the book's final movement: 21 untitled poems in tercets, including the poems featured here.

These 21 poems combine the journal-like quality of the shortest poems in the book with the more substantial qualities of the longer poems. They embody a deft, light touch while pursuing serious, sometimes unsettling ideas. Many of the hallmarks of Šalamun's work appear in these poems: his preoccupation with family and friends, the collision of the surreal and the quotidian, his fascination (and, at times, conflict) with God, the strangeness of the natural world, his embrace of both the absurd and the terrible. The poems' style and form contribute to a breeziness, an easing off the impulse for rational interpretation, encouraging the reader to glide along the text rather than grapple with it. But the poems invite multiple readings, as new readings illuminate new connections, new depths.

My approach to translating Šalamun's poetry entails being as literal as possible (which in his case generally means avoiding the temptation to over-interpret, domesticate, smooth out rough patches, or explain away ambiguities) while producing a poem in English that carries some residue of the original. I want my translations to function as poems in English (not as transcripts of a poetic text) while not necessarily appearing to have been written in English: ideally, they are parallel primary texts that depend on—and are imbued with—the original but also stand on their own.

TOMAŽ ŠALAMUN : Four Poems from *Falcon*

Jesus Christ
is black and red.
Everything

human is
in him. We are
all worried and

wherever
we move,
worry comes

and assaults us.
Just like Jesus
Christ.

Please, let's
get along.
This isn't

an analogue,
but the same
flesh.

Perfection is
always circular, not
pointed.

A triangle is
really circular, which is why
it brings such peace.

Sometimes it seems
like history
is stretching out an arm.

This isn't true.
History doesn't have
that power.

Look at
the jungle! Look
at the house!

The house
is God's
cube.

Catastrophes
are in blue.
The explosions

above us
are in red. Waaah,
waaah builds

in gold
and green. Yellow
calms.

The whisk goes
up the hill and says:
little bees,

lay
eggs. The lake dwellers
are yelling

in the hurricane.
The wild ducks
forecast it.

The wild
ducks were
protecting us.

I am
infinitely
free.

All my
thinking
is

technical.
Like the thinking
of trees.

Birds
think
only

technically
when flying, the same as
angels.

Translated from the Slovenian by Brian Henry

KATE WEINBERG

Goating

FAMILY LORE BLAMES SARAH SHWARZ for its bad-luck blood. Sarah Shwarz, before she became Sarah Horowitz, in Sambor, when it was still part of Poland, before it was annexed to Ukraine and renamed Sambir, before it was assigned ghetto status, before weaponed guards with long gray faces protected its barricades, before Wannsee, before Everyone's faces became long and gray, anemic, dyspeptic, chronic. When walls were still being built and before they began to fall. When Jews still attended dances in synagogues and small, bloodbrick town halls stacked to hold them in when no one else would, to make them each other's. Of each other, by each other, for each other. To couple them and only them, to mingle their DNA into a single stew with only one or two strains into which to dip one's spoon.

Sarah and Sol. Sol and Sarah. Sol a slickster, single dark curl like the north star, pulsing at the center of his forehead. Sarah all crimped waist and stacked—kind of chest you could rest a challah on. Mega-tits a poorly-kept secret beneath the tease of a full-cover dress—one of those Eastern European peasant-dealies. Two hottie bodies, magnetized to each other at the dessert table in the corner of The Bais Yakov Dance Hall for Jewish Youth. Eight lights of the Hanukkah menorah blazing. The oily miracle! The Maccabees fought but Sol and Sarah were easy with each other, for each other, by each other, to each other. Sol held her hand the whole first time they did it, kissing a trail from forehead to shmundie on a blanket by the Dnister river.

Sarah was seventeen when they married, seventeen-and-five-months when Freida bloomed out of her (feet-first) on the bathroom floor in Sarah's parents' flat, where they lived. Seventeen and nine months when she watched her parents and younger sister get pogrom'd in the street by Polish soldiers, mobbed and shouting. Seventeen and nine months when she, Sol and Freida (babe in arms) boarded trains and trains and trains and, finally, the Red Star Line from Antwerp to Baltimore (Bal'mer) City. Nineteen when the letter arrived from cousin Yessie (also escaped) explaining that her aunts and uncles and older brother, Yakov, hadn't made it, either. Nineteen when Ester was born. Twenty-one when Chaia. Twenty-one-and-a-half when Sol had gambled good enough and long enough to open a tiny grocery store on the corner of Eutaw and Whitelock. Twenty-one-and-a-half when they left Jossel's house—Sol's cousin—and moved into the cramped two-bedroom apartment above the store. Thirty-nine when Rebbe Moskovitz blessed the union of Freida and Josef Abramson at B'nai Israel. Forty-one when Ester became Lichtenstein. Forty-two when Chaia's foot accidentally slipped its satin pump during the cracking of the glass, blood goozing out from the arch. (Chaia still became Blum, but the marriage remained permanently tainted.) Forty-two when her first granddaughter, Ava, was born. Forty-four when Stuart. Forty-five, David. Forty-five, Joseph. Forty six, Linda. Forty-nine, Deborah. Fifty-one when people in town began to whisper on her sudden and excessive hairiness. Fifty-three when the hairiness crept onto her face and neck and her nose began to spread and lengthen into something closer to a snout. Fifty-three when she stopped speaking, as though she had forgotten how. Fifty-four when her body, drained of blood from the wrists, was found by her youngest daughter, Chaia.

All the family ever knew about it—about any of it—was that Grandpa Sol had to sell the grocery store to pay for the funeral at Levinson's and the plot at Oheb Shalom. Everyone knew that bribes back then were exorbitantly high to bury a suicide. What they didn't know, what was never spoke aloud, is they were even higher to bury a woman who was halfway to becoming a goat.

•

At fifteen years, eleven months and thirteen days, Jamie finds a Rorschach of blood in her underwear. She's changing into her grub-around clothes for Painting and Drawing II—it's canvas-stretch and gesso day. She glances around the stall, wondering if she should cry or laugh or fist-pump into the fetid high-school-bathroom air. She whispers a little *yesssss* into the wad of t.p. in her fist.

Dr. Pritzger has been monitoring her for years (at J's mother's behest) at the eating disorder clinic at Hopkins. Taking her blood. Forcing her to drink high-caloric Boost shakes that taste like chalk (chalk mixed with shit, which she swills around her mouth and spits out when no one's watching). She's told J if she doesn't bleed by the time she's sixteen, they'll have to take more drastic measures (cryptic bitch). As though bleeding were a button Jamie could press on the, on like the *machine* of her body. It is literally the worst. And she has recovered (!), mostly, from the years spent eating nothing but the sticky pinkish gunk in the center of strawberry pop-tarts. She eats *lunch meat* now. Bread, bananas, FRENCH FRIES (ten-to-fifteen, from Kristin's pack, in the McDonald's parking lot after school on Fridays). It's a boring story. She eats. She eats sugar, grease, salt.

Mari has started puking after lunch in the center stall, not caring who hears. At least when Jamie'd been doing the damn thing, she'd been discreet, and she'd almost never puked stuff up. As soon as people find out, that's when they make you stop (everyone knows that). But Mari's young for her age, and only taking honors or standard classes (which is a petty thing to bring up, but it's true). Jamie is in all

G.T. Next year, she'll try for AP English, History, Art. Have her own little studio, to paint in, or sleep in. To decorate with sketches of naked people and plants and macramé, like Anaïs, or Lindy, or Antonia.

Next year she'll get a boyfriend. Give a blowjob. When they're in love, they'll do it. They'll do it every day. In the darkroom, like all the art kids do. She has one in mind. She's been trying not to creep on him after school, watching his soccer practices from the bleachers. Been trying to play it cool as he lifts his muscle shirt to wipe the sweat from his forehead at the end of a play.

The bell for next period—(ha)—trills. She has no *menstrual* (the word makes her mouth-lip curl) pads and has never (as-of-yet), officially, fully, totally put anything up her v., so she shoves the t.p. wad in her undies and prays she won't bleed through. There is some humiliation even time can't undo. Everyone knows that.

•

BY THE TIME an undeniably bristly fur begins creeping up Jamie's mother, Deborah's, legs, by the time the fingers of her right hand begin to fuse, gently, together, they've got a name for it. Ziegewerden, coined by a doctor in Cologne in the eighties, though the disease is shrouded enough that most people have never heard of it. It's a name that might have been offered sooner had anyone known it was an actual phenomenon, "a condition often passed between generations by way of rogue DNA, the origins of which are often epigenetic adaptations born of an individual's physiological response to trauma" (Mandel, Robert. *When Genes Stop Fitting*. Bethesda: Goldear, 2005) and not a one-off, beleaguering strangeness. A name that is useful only as a means of acknowledging the existence of something, but that promises nothing further.

Mandel later goes on to say that, "in certain in-the-shadows conditions, like Ziegewerden (or, "Goating," as it is referred to colloquially in certain parts of the world), an individual may carry the biomarker for the disease but never become symptomatic . . . From what we are beginning to understand, the gene that causes Ziegerwerden may be expressed or depressed depending on an individual's exposure to traumatic events. While this may provide a sense of relief to those at risk, the fact that individuals have little control over the trauma to which they'll be exposed, or other genetic and developmental factors that dictate their response to that trauma, means no one with the biomarker is truly in the clear."

Several pages beyond, he writes, "[a]t present, Goating is a disease very far from understanding and thus very far from a cure. It is a disease that traffics, primarily, in relentlessness. In the absence of hope. It is this, beyond anything else, that places it among the most devastating conditions that currently afflict humankind." (Mandel, 46-47)

In the appendix, (among other things), Mandel provides web address to an article he deems "as hopeful as this gets." It details the story of an anthropology professor in Tennessee who began goating at fifty-five. Just before becoming entirely quadrupedal, she arranged for her recent-ex-husband to score a bottle of liquid pentobarbital sodium and gather her closest friends, her daughter, the ex-husband, for a proper send-off. While they told stories of her life in the living room, she lapped a cocktail of pento and red wine from a bowl on her bedroom floor, fell into a brief coma, and died.

Mandel's own father, a kid of the Great Depression and a vet of Korea with permanent purpledark-circles under the eyes, began goating at seventy-five. He was placed in a home with outdoor stables several states away by seventy-nine but was not pronounced physically dead until eighty-three. Mandel admits in interviews he put his father away to avoid the indelible trauma inherent in watching him transform from man-who-raised-him into full-blown goat.

Mandel took his own life with pentobarbitol at fifty, two years after the book was published, a month after his first (and last) interview on *60 Minutes*. The men who buried him said they'd never seen a hairier set of ankles.

·

DEBORAH, DEB, LITTLE Debbie, Deb-bra, Doobie, Mama, Mom, Moo. She is trying to make a batch of chocolate chip cookies for her children, for when they home. Arrive, home. From school—where they live. During the day. They live at school. The go to school. They come home. They live at home. With her. And Dan. With the cat. They all live at home.

Deborah scuffs around the kitchen trying to reach for things. Deborah, Deb, Little Debbie, Deb-bra, Doobie, Mama, Mom, Moo. Words. And names. Names for her. Her—the names her'd been called and was trying to hold on to. Words were getting stuck in her throat now, and in her head, like cud she had to chew so by the time she spoke them they were tangled, full of spit. But her names, she will keep them. She will keep them even as she drops the bag of King Arthur Flour and white dust scatters, clouds spuming up.

Even coughing is hard—she gurgles the stuff out, it slides sticky down the hairs on her chin. Chinny chin chin. Nursery Rhyme. Jacob liked that one when he was tiny—three little pigs, smoke stacks, houses tumbling down. She pries open a drawer and knocks out a measuring cup, begins scooping floor-flour into it until the cup is brimming. Scoots out a bowl, angles it in.

She will make these cookies. She will. She's found a method. Does the butter the same way, the sugar, the chocolate chips. Shimmies them to the tile floor, rips the packaging with teeth or foot, scoops and slides.

Smart woman. Class president two years in a row. Deborah. Deb. Deb-bra. Doobie.

Linda started calling her that after she caught Little Deb stealing from her weed jar in ninth grade. It was the sixties. Big sisters owed it to their Littles—that's what Deb thought. And then their mother found out, said *this kind of shit is for the goyem!* Slapped Deb with the bottom end of a high heel across the cheek. Blood, a raised line of scab in her school picture, a permanent scar. On her face. Deb—not Linda. Linda the first, the golden. Deb the baby that made her fat, she always reminded her. *Oh, the* figure *I had,* she used to say. *Before you oozed out.*

Deb called her Chaia after that, and Fat Chaia behind her back. She lost the privileges of Mom. No skinny baby could make a woman that mammoth. Chaia had recorded the stats in Deb's baby book—she'd seen them many times over. *Deborah Tovah Blum. Height: 17.5 in. Weight: 6 lbs 1 oz.* The other three hundred were on her.

Fat Chaia was a *depressive,* and a convenient one at that. She'd get it together for Linda's recitals, Linda's softball games, Linda's proms, Linda's dates. For Deb's, she was always "*resting—don't bother me*" behind a closed door. The whole family said she'd been different, before she found her mother's body. But Deb was only five when that happened and had no memories of her mother having been anything but what she was. Fat Chaia. Wide and rude. Spiteful, manipulative, scarring.

Pop only came home from the pharmacy when he had to. Deb's pop. She didn't blame him—he kissed her goodnight, cleaned up Chaia's messes, drove Deb to friend's houses, picked her up, too, made her hot toddies when she was sick (*it'll burn that flu right out of you, pup,* he'd say, his big hand testing the heat of her forehead). Deb loved her Pop. Would have died without her Pop, then. Fat Chaia would have been happy to let her go. Maybe then she could have got her "figure" back.

And when her Papa did die (a coronary event) when she was eighteen, she did not recover. She told Fat Chaia she considered herself an orphan. Which was true. And Linda said, *oh, Doobie. She's not going to start loving you just because you reject her, now.* And Deb missed her Pop so much she could have filled a concert hall with Yahrzeit candles and it wouldn't have even covered an inch of her grief.

SHE realizes she's—Deb, Little Debbie, Deb-bra—she's been mashing the ingredients together hard, so hard the chocolate chips aren't chips anymore. Flat. Chocolate disks. And she misses her Pop. Her Papa. And the buttons to turn the oven on are so so small. She dips her head into the bowl of mashed stuff—sugar clumping with butter, flour clumping flour, clubbing, clumping, all of it a mash-mess on her feet (why is she using her feet? Debra asks herself, but cannot answer, just knows it's the only way)—and begins to lick. Sugar against her tongue feels good. She thinks of how she'll shape the cookies, with her hands and feet that aren't working like they should (and Dan says it's just arthritis, but) but. She loses her thought-train, the sugar is good. The *butter* is good. She's never let herself sit on the ground and eat dough before. Her mother's size always a pox upon her mind, body. Having control meant she could not blame her babies for anything. Her whiskers are sodden now with granulated sugar-butter, flour sticking to her chin-fur.

Little Deb, Deb-bra, Doobie is having a *good* time. Three little pigs. Jamie loved cookies before she became an anorexic. Jacob, sweet boy, good boy, best boy. Jacob—little Prince—will gobble them up.

•

DAN ONLY AGREES to take her in for testing because Other People have begun to notice. Other People have been pulling him aside at parties, family gatherings, at the Safeway off of Owings Mills Boulevard, to discuss his wife with him—There's something different, the Other People say. Her ears—have you really not noticed her ears?

But it had been so subtle, and so slow-growing, that he hadn't. Not really. Because when you see someone so often, Dan reasons, you accommodate their incremental differences until you become blind to them. The picture is forming and you are watching it form and so you almost miss the places where dust has begun to gather, where the canvas has begun to fray. Or, in this case, to fur.

She is theirs—Dan's, Jamie's, Jacob's, Midge the cat's. And so they forget to recognize the way her ears have begun to soften and down-turn, how the edges of them, of her, are beginning to grow almost downy. They chalk up the fuzz forming on her extremities to The Aging Process (she'd had them late—thirty-nine with Jamie. Forty-one with Jacob.) Menopause. Hormonal Imbalance. Estrogen Depletion. Too Much Time Spent Indoors. Turpentine Fumes.

And, plus: No. Just, No. It was not a thing that happened. It was not a thing that happened to women in their fifties, living with their working husbands and school-age children in neat middle-class suburban houses that did not smell of piss, as his own house had smelled, his grandfather groaning upstairs, wetting himself prodigiously.

It was not a thing that could happen to *her*. She who he met at his own garage sale outside the apartment complex on Cold Spring, one long dark braid down her back. She who'd said, while handing over the $1.50 for his mother's old glass pitcher, *You better not be moving far.* (He wasn't moving at all, in fact; just wanted to unburden himself of some of the physical accumulations of living; and, make a small profit while doing so.) She who lived in *the same apartment complex all this time* and he hadn't even known it, ding that he was. She who stunned him alive at twenty-two after what felt like a lifetime spent nerdy, bad-with-girls, bad-of-skin, charming but too nervous to do anything with it. She who read his chart and proclaimed his Mars in the 7th house meant he'd be a passionate lover. And so, he was. With her animal hunger moving down his body, around his hardness, teasing out his wildness to match her own. Once, they'd even taken Quaaludes. Eve of Yom Kippur, his office closed the next day. He'd asked if he could put himself in her asshole. And she'd said yes. And he'd cum before submerging even the tip. And it worried him now he'd somehow done something, then. Set some terrible thing in motion. They were supposed to be repenting and they'd done that instead. And she was the first love—the only love. His.

And she was *careful*. With everything. Weighed her food on a small kitchen scale. Maintained the integrity of pairs of shoes *ad infinitum*, lined up just so in her closet. Kept everything neatly hung, starched, smelling of new leather and dry-cleaning. Went to fairs in other states and brought back gemstones and Swarovski crystals in small silk bags, cold, gleaming Fabergé egg-replicas, small porcelain women in Victorian dresses (for Jamie, always for Jamie). Lined these women up in rows: tidy, particular. Put notes each day in the bag lunches of their children, even though they were teenagers now (Jamie particularly salty). Sometimes included stickers. Recorded her own weight each morning in a small notepad kept hidden in her bedside table, a long spine of numbers by which to mete out self-punishment or reward.

He'd tried to hide the notepad from her a few times, but it always became a fight they had. He'd said, *what if Jamie finds it? What if she's already found it? Daughters learn from their mothers, they watch, they imitate. What if that's why?* And Debbie'd sat on the bed, notepad in lap, staring at her hands a whole minute before she'd begun ripping out the pages. *You think that's going to fix it?* She'd asked, forehead-vein pulsing. *Is that going to make it go away?*

He regretted the whole thing now. Thinking her body was his. Blaming her for a thing—a little girl—they'd made but couldn't control. She'd never brought it up again after that. And everything had returned to normal.

He decided that This Past Year, she was just tired. She'd worked hard rearing, raising their children, crafting, feeding the cat, working the extra odd job around holidays. She deserved Rest. That's why she sometimes struggled to stay upright, or to speak. Most people got hairier as they got older—their noses grew, their ears. It was Normal Stuff. Her hands were just Arthritic from all the artwork. The subtle curve of her spine Late-Onset Scoliosis.

It's not until the specialist they finally come to see—after months of putting it off, after several rounds of blood tests, an MRI, a CAT, a PET—calls them back into her office and gives them a name, gives them The Name (the one they hadn't even considered), that Dan looks at his wife's hand in his and finally notices. That her fingers have fused, and shortened, and hardened, a stark cleft dividing them into two points. That her palm is rough, and dark, the whole appendage capped in a stiff fur distinctly unlike regular, human arm-hair. Distinctly unlike *Debbie's* arm hair. He tightens his grip around his wife's hand, understanding that it's not a hand any longer. It's a hoof.

•

I DUNNO, JACOB says, when Ms. Seltzer (aka The Seltz) asks him to define the Standard Deviation of a board-full of numbers during Algebra. He pushes his fingers through his scalp. I—I really don't know.

He's flicking the half-moon of his thumbnail across his desk, playing a personal game of desk-soccer. Jacob always knows things. He knows this. But he's sick of being the Kid Who Knows. Wants to be the Kid Who is Really Good at Soccer, like the boy Jamie has a crush on. Vlad. Who's so good at soccer they let him stay on the team, even though he cuts class every day and is failing three subjects. Who their family "hosted" right after Vlad's family immigrated ten years ago, because Ukraine was still on board with ending its "Jewish problem," when Jacob was only four. Vlad, who—for whatever reason—gives him a peace sign whenever they pass in the halls, whenever he *is* there, which makes Jacob a little bit sweaty.

But Jacob's not Vlad. He's the Skinny Kid Who Nailed His Haftorah Portion last year so precisely that even the rabbi, after, said: *Shit, kid. Go play outside sometime.* He's the Kid Who's Always Had One Friend (also named Jacob, but who goes by Jake), but he wants to be the Kid Who Moves Between (social strata, tables in the cafeteria, girls at the Homecoming dance). He wants to be the Kid Who Kisses Girls in the Hallway. More like his sister (well, boys in her case, as far as he knows). Or like Delke Pentwaith, who somehow manages to straddle both leads in the school musicals (girl-kissing in-built) and point guard (male bonding, lithe+muscles+showers) and thus never get called gay. He didn't exactly know what was wrong with being gay, but he knew it was somehow correlated with 'loser' so he didn't want to be it.

You really *don't know.* The Seltz squints at him, suspicious. He keeps staring at his thumbnail on the desk. Who can help Jacob? Seltz asks the class.

But No One can help Jacob. They all already know this. He is the Kid Who Helps Everyone Else. *But*, he thinks, a glimmer of sweat rising against his collar, *not today.*

Frowning and small-handed, The Seltz puts up a slide which tells them the answer, which Jacob already knew, which, suddenly, feels like a cruel, stupid thing to be learning about—*deviation*, things going off-course—even though no teacher at school—no one at all—knows about his mom because he hasn't told them and because none of it even makes sense. He hasn't even told Jake, who has finally stopped asking why Jacob insists they always go to Jake's house from now on, even though Jacob's house is bigger and doesn't smell like cigarettes and there is always better food in the fridge (or, there *was*, when Mom still did the grocery shopping.)

In the seven months since he's found out Mom is Goating, everything's taken on a shivery, unreal quality. He hadn't been looking closely before because he hadn't needed to, but now he sees everything is gauzy and thin. See-through.

There are things he didn't realize he'd ever have to witness. Mom in his sock drawer, nibbling holes in the heels with her weirdly-long bottom teeth. Walking in on his father helping her bathe, lathering the hairiness of her back and middle with oatmeal horse shampoo. The day he came home from school, just before Winter break, and she was (inexplicably) coated in sugar-butter, an empty metal bowl upturned, the cat licking flour and egg-yolk from the kitchen floor beside her.

Jacob's feeling antsy, restless; *reckless*. He raises his hand for the bathroom, forgets to take the hall pass off the board when he leaves. Walks through the math wing, past the bathrooms, the vending machines, pulls his striped shirt out of his jeans (fuck the tuck!) heads down the science wing stairs, past the cafeteria, down the history hall, past the front office and out the side entrance.

He's never, ever done this before. Walked right out, in the middle of third period, or any period. He's cutting, which makes him a Cutter, he realizes. And his mother is slowly dying (Dad hesitated to tell them how long; *the specialist*, he said, *says it's different for everyone*. But someone on Reddit said *six-to-eight years*, and someone else qualified, *six-to-eight* horrific, undignified, barely conscious, inhumane *years*.) His chest and face go clammy, heart thumping, as he walks through the parking lot toward the McDonalds on Fairmont, looking over his shoulder a thousand times. But no one's following him, no one's watching, tapping their foot in disappointment. He hears no footsteps in hot pursuit, no Jake shouting, *what the butt are you* doing, *man?*, no Principal Trillisk bellowing, *I'm disappointed in you, Jacob Katz*. All the stuff he thought happened to Cutters.

All he hears are sirens going off at the detention center up the hill and cars shushing by on York Road, traffic en route to Towson Mall beginning to congest, sedans beep-beeping their way into the leftmost lane.

It's *easy*. So fucking easy! (Jacob makes a mental note to begin cursing with greater frequency, out loud. It's something fearless people do, people with nothing to lose, which now includes him.)

ONCE he gets to the McDonald's parking lot, he's not sure what to do except make sure no one sees him. He pulls a raincoat from his bag and puts it on, hood up.

He's got two dollars and fifty cents jangling around the front pocket of his book bag (it was his turn to buy Cool Ranch Doritos, a Hershey's bar and a Mountain Dew for him and Jake to share during break in World History). But now he's free to buy whatever (the fuck?) he wants. So he'll waltz in and get, maybe, two orders of fries and a McFlurry. And eat them? Somewhere? Up York Road? In the parking lot outside Just Puppies, where Jamie sometimes liked to drag him, after school, to stare at inbred dogs in—

—Yo, Little Katz! A voice—his name. (*Fuck*). He clenches, starts walking forward like he hadn't heard (shit). A hand on his shoulder. He turns.

Vlad! (There's the peace sign.) Jacob's heart doing triple-steps. Sweat blooming from his armpits.

Dude, Little Katz. Vlad looks at the raincoat, looks at the sky, holds his palm out like he's expecting something to land in it. You know something I don't? Vlad laughs, takes a pack of Camels from the pocket of his soccer shorts. Still got a hint of slav in his voice, even ten years in. You playing the hook, Little K?

Jacob pulls down the hood, tries to act casual. Takes a cigarette awkwardly between his fingers when Vlad offers it to him. He guesses it's not a real Camel—loose brown shreds of tobacco rolled up in some approximation of "cigarette." Yeah, Jacob says, trying to puff out what skinny chest he has. I—really wanted some fucking fries.

Fuckin' right, man, Vlad says, giving a high five. He takes a long drag, looks at Jacob with big, serious green (more like *aqua*, deep-sea kelp) eyes. I've been seeing a lot of your sister down here, too. She's kind of wigging out right now, you know?

Yeah, I guess so, Jacob says. But, really, he feels like he hardly sees his sister anymore. He'd always heard crisis brought people closer but he and Dad and Jamie all avoid talking about it so much the house has gone almost silent.

He puts the (fucking) cigarette between his lips. Vlad lights it and Jacob tries to take the smoke into his lungs, but it hurts. So he takes real superficial puffs and holds them in his mouth for a count of two and then releases them, hoping this passes as smoking. It hits him that he probably looks pretty cool right now. That he's smoking a cigarette with Vlad, who's a star athlete on the soccer team and has crazy bulging calf muscles and probably a trail of hair running from his navel to his dick. He probably has lots of pubic hair, thick and dark. He wishes he wasn't thinking of Vlad's pubic hair, but he is and no one ever has to know.

She sent me the article, Vlad says.

Jacob shakes his head. (Little puff. Hold it in. One, two. Blow it out.) Article?

About the woman, in Memphis? With the same thing as your mom? Apparently, there's a whole book about it, too. He takes another deep drag and exhales over his right shoulder. Maaaan. I remember goin' to your house for Hanukkah parties when we were fresh off the boat. Your mom was always, like, dusting shit and baking, and lifting all the kids in the air and making us sing Hebrew songs and dance around in circles. I remember thinking, like, damn, these people are so *Jewish*, when you weren't. You were just American, so you could do whatever you wanted. Vlad pauses. Hey—how's she doing? Your momma?

Jacob's stomach seizes. Hates talking about his mom. Hates hearing about how she used to be. She's—he hesitates. He doesn't want to talk about the past three times he's quietly cleaned up her shit on the kitchen floor, or the times he's heard his dad run for new towels from the linen closet in the middle of the night, or the times he's heard Jamie screaming into her pillow behind a closed door, or the times he's heard his dad crying into his hands behind the closed double-doors of his study.

I don't know, Jacob says. She's. She's not really my mom anymore.

It's the first time he's said it out loud. And it makes him feel like the worst kid alive.

•

DEBORAH, DEB, LITTLE Debbie, Deb-bra, Doobie, Mama, Mom, Moo. Deb. Doobie. Mom. Momma. Moo. Little Deb. Her names. Her. Her's. Dooooooooobie doob. Doobster. Dibdibdib. She wanted to call out for Jamie in the other room before she let the water leave her body, but she couldn't reach. Glottal throat. The song her Pop sung. Strangers in the night do do do do do. Her daughter's sweater in her mouth, the long strands of her hair. Her daughter screaming, no, no, fuck, oh, fuck. Cotton on the edges of teeth. The bigness of the tongue.

•

THE BOOTH-PLEATHER at the Towson diner is sticky against Jamie's thighs but Vlad's fingers are resting on top of them beneath the table and her vag has started like, pulsing, or something. So she can ignore the leg sweat a while. She can ignore that they're in the smoking section. She can ignore Jacob resting his cigarette in the ashtray, staring back at them from across the table, shoveling bits of waffle into his mouth almost viciously. She can almost, almost ignore (for exactly three seconds at a time) the fact they're about to drive to some freaky Russian mafia dude's house in Reservoir Hill to collect a bottle of liquid pentobarbital sodium smuggled fresh from a pharmacy, hopefully somewhere very far away.

She can't ignore that it feels complicated and wrong that she wants Jacob to find a reason to leave and Vlad to press himself against her in the booth and put two-maybe-three fingers inside of her. *Right now.* With everything else. It doesn't make sense, but she is used to that now. Holding two opposing realities in her skull.

When her mother nudged into her room last night, approached her bed and began chewing at her hair, Jamie decided it was okay for her to find this both very funny and very awful.

When she found pamphlets in the drawer of her father's desk for farms in Pennsylvania, Virginia, Rhode Island that promised *a safe and respectful place for your loved one to live out their days with a team of 24-hour caretakers and all the hay they can eat!*, she decided it was okay to both cut them up, and burn them over the gas flame of the stove.

Vlad glances between them—Jamie's untouched bowl of tomato soup, the sticky remnants of Jacob's waffle. Glances at the time on the cracked screen of his Nokia. We should go, no?

No, Jamie thinks, watching his Adam's apple bob as he swallows. We should stay here, maybe forever.

But they pay the bill. And walk out the door, sun beginning to dip toward the city, down down down into the toxic mouth of the Chesapeake.

WE don't have to actually use it, Jacob says when they're halfway there, driving slower than normal on 83 South. Right?

Jamie turns from the passenger seat. Watches as her little brother's face screws up in an effort not to cry. She's shaking like she's cold but she's not cold; it's almost June. Of course we don't, she says, softly. We don't have to do anything. But she's thinking of Mandel's book, discovered (also) in her father's desk drawer several months ago. She's thinking of how long a person can live like how her mother is living, getting worse and worse and worse. She's thinking of how quickly she changed (*a fast transition doesn't mean a faster death!* the doctor told them at her last appointment, thinking this was reassuring.) She's thinking of how many times (11) Mandel said "no one with agency would ever *choose* to continue living with this disease." She's thinking of the time her mother flipped her shit after Jamie'd borrowed her favorite white jacket and returned it with a miniscule nacho-cheese stain on the sleeve. Of the birthday cakes she'd spend hours decorating, every line piped clean and precise, the Halloween costumes she stayed up all night sewing. She's thinking of every time she ran away (4) and every time her mother knew exactly where to find her (4), beneath the back deck, covered in the same ratty picnic blanket, her soft hand meeting the shell of Jamie's back, rubbing it gently. She's thinking of her mother's willowy body at the top of the stairs, the silhouette of her smallness in the dark, her black hair in its reliable bob, organized and untangled, even fresh from sleep. The trips she and her mother had taken to New York around Christmastime—mother/daughter—everything frosty and golden and vibrating around them as her mother led Jamie into the basement of that Japanese department store she liked for afternoon tea and tiny crustless sandwiches cut into triangles. The delicate ceramic objects they would finger side-by-side on the shelves, breathing in the soft, clean smells of cotton and planter soil and jasmine. She's thinking (she's hoping) that for all the years she'd decided she and her mother didn't understand each other even one iota, she'd been wrong. Maybe it was that they'd been so similar they'd become almost blind to each other. This worries Jamie, too. The fact that her mother's body built her body, her blood. That her mother's blood flows through her and occupies half the space of her DNA. That inside of her, right now, is a tide of information, invisibly coded, holding her future tight in its dark fist.

Vlad signals to move into the right lane; their exit is coming. I can call this dude up, he says. Tell him we changed our mind. He'll probably still want the cash, but, we can figure it out. I can talk to him.

Jamie swallows against the fist-sized lump in her throat. No, she says. We're getting it.

It had been hard to find. Vlad said all Russians had a mafia connection somewhere down the line, and she guessed he wasn't joking because he found her in the hall outside of physics three weeks ago and told her. He'd found a guy who knew a guy who knew a dude about to make a run to somewhere sketchy. He put the order in for them. And then it came. And here it was. Ready for pick-up.

She looks at her little bro again in the rearview. Jacob's sniffling, checking out the broken sidewalks, the bent street signs and bullet-holed windows of painted ladies and old churches crumbling into themselves, trees in the distance fattening with gold-green leaves. Their great-grandparents had owned a grocery store around here once; she knew that. Great-Grandpa Sol had to sell it after Grandma Chaia found the body.

•

A SMALL BROWN bottle in a small white bag. That's all it is. A maraca, shaking beneath Jamie's arm as she clutches it to her ribcage, just below the heart, the heart her mother built for her sixteen years ago in the dark of her body. An instrument. Breath-stopper. Life-ender. Miracle. Murder weapon. Gentler than a gunshot. Slower-acting. To allow space, time for their mother to reach into Whatever Comes Next—the tide rushing forward, taking what the body holds, letting the body go, letting it go. Preserver of memory, of what was, of what will never again be. Their mother is already gone. The maraca of pills shakes near Jamie's heart, or maybe it's the other way around.

A possibility. An option. A choice. A just-in-case. That's all it is.

•

DEB. DEBORAH. DEBORAH Tovah Blum. Little Debbie. Doo-Doo-Doobie. Human on the DL. She doesn't see her mother in her dreams. Only her Pop. His skin a constellation of red dots. The smooth green skin of Lvov, Dnister river dyed bloody red. The long arms of her husband. Her children, blooming from the center of her, the vernix coating their skin like cottage cheese. Jamie didn't eat, even then. The breast a far-away place. Their eyes locking when she finally latched. The cool dark room where they got to be quiet with each other. Jacob's nightmares. He worried he'd die one day. He worried no one would be there to meet him. Pop at her forehead. *Don't worry, Pup.* Pop at her forehead. *It'll burn the bad right out of you.*

She had everything to say. But she could say nothing now. Only gurgle. Nicker. Bleat.

•

JAMIE CLIMBS INTO bed with her mother when they get home from the city. Her father is in his office, banker's lamp on, spine of gold light between the double-doors. The small brown bottle in the small white bag is tucked deep in the back of her closet. Breath-taker. Miracle. Murder Weapon. They don't have to use it. They never have to use it.

Her mother's breathing is heavy, her thick legs tremble. Jamie makes herself a small spoon, tucks herself into the curve of her mother's body. She wants to smell her, beneath the animal fur. She wants to find the smell of her mother's skin. What remains. What still exists. Her mother's body, that built her body, her blood. Her mother's ears twitch. Without thinking, she puts a hand on her mother's forehead. She rubs her snout. She kisses her closed eyelids.

VIRGINIA KONCHAN

Theory of Mind

If I told you how much time I spent
emailing those the rest of the world

has forgotten, you would be appalled.
5 hours a day, usually. Sometimes 8.

In all honesty it is the rejection of self
that has ruined me and my career.

I: a drainage pipe, a catheter.
I: formlessless preceding form,

pathetic little realm. I am astounded
at the result: my utter failure to exist.

You have to believe in an enemy force:
elsewise, to whom could you attribute

your inability to earn a living wage,
survive, be happy, or merely be?

Being: an unnecessary extravagance.
Bonjour, tristesse. My taxidermic body,

too, thrills me. I love people whom the world
hasn't ruined, but I love people whom the world

has ruined more. I wanted to put language in its place.
I wanted, when I said "metaphysical," for you to agree.

It is the mannerism of an object to be devoid
of thought. A feeling is an idea with wings.

Beyond discourse, debate, interpretation:
far beyond all centuries and their decrees.

Beyond vulva, mouth, joy, delight,
or whatever those pink things mean.

SOPHIE KLAHR & COREY ZELLER

Aim

You scrape whole meals off the plate the way a doctor shaves at a bone. You see the sky
    as a disjoined thing;
unset; needing to be put back into place. You see that blue crescent of space and are as
    blank and black
as a nightingale's eye; as the Mojave at night; as the reflection of a tree inside the blade
    of a saw. It might
as well be hunger. Which is what, really, but the knowledge that everything is filled
    with itself.
How you walk into a room and people look at you like an elevator opening. Their faces
    saying: *I'll wait*
for the next one. Their faces saying: *how could I possibly fit with all those people inside?*

MARC McKEE

I'm having a weird time with my many too many tongues

Think about putting your hand down now
on anything, even now

knowing a little more, think you, think
on how many anythings

you would like to reassure.
The vocabulary we had before

we still have, but even
at its most elastic and aware

it could not move its fingers
over enough of this animal

to begin to make out its face, for instance
does it have just the one. Now

we pause for a short advertisement.
If this advertisement was a fish

it would be a minnow. But it is always
this way. No ditch you dig will stay

dug. You can't teach Shakespeare
so Shakespeare stays taught.

The minnow explodes into many
other exploding minnows. The skin

of an orange becomes candy
or dirt according to the degree

of human imposition upon
circumstances and human imposition

upon circumstances is miraculous,
a grace, a wild menace, a murder

in progress, a murder of progress,
the most delicious wedge salad.

Where are we without a desire
for a lovely unlikelihood

and a dream of saying it into being.
How many new hands must we grow

for our imagining to give account
of this rough beast now born,

to say how we brought it to heel,
singing like gutted fools

at its lengthening cost, the disappearing
coasts—what can be brought to heel

now is a sad question. How many
cunning tongues to steer through

to a loose congregation
of newborn islands

striking out for each other,
struggling to use all these spears

like oars.

JAMES ELLENBERGER

Scars Poetica

We've done our best to carbon date the poem.
We've force fed it grievances and greatness.
We've excised its pain-fat liver, thwacked it wet
on a serving tray. Here, a poem, o Glutton Lord.

The heart is likewise thwacked. An opus. A gelding.
A soft shriveled weight in the palm, then jostling
in dirty wicker with the others, fresh curls plucked
from the field as if from a daydream of burning.

The poem must be removed. Little else can be saved,
sadly. There's no time for laughing gas or modesty,
only the preponderance of which hunk will weigh
favorably against a feather. The amphitheater

is an eye rapturous with irony. Those in attendance
can't see the fire being scooped out of our bellies
with both hands. Because they can't see the fire
they think it's all marvelous. They think we're dancing.

Still Life with a Thing for Vore

Look, the painter's catacombed
the peaches; there's a brain
buried in each, solipsizing.

The pit has a vision of flesh:
endless sun-sweet fields
in all directions: the snugness

of dead center, it's enough.
Eons pass in halcyonic amber,
a cacophony of inert wings.

There are days when the fly,
though fixed, appears to tremble
and the ossified brain views it

as a sign from a past life. Distant,
a patch of freshly scalloped light:
it looks like lost love's face,

no, like something is taking a bite.

MATTY LAYNE GLASGOW

hyperphagia,
or euxoa auxiliaris

Your hunger is always shrouded in darkness, hatched on the underside of a mustard leaf or in the cheatgrass's damp shade where you consume your birthplace, all the thick green shine of spring lost in larval appetite: a month-long binge, a nightly plague, your swelling thorax. Full, you burrow in the wet soil, in amber stillness, dormant but not unchanged by a fortnight in the underworld. Perhaps you tremble as you emerge, as new cravings rustle the wings of second coming. In summer, you love to be high, & your desire takes flight beneath the new moon—wings all shadow in starlight over the once-vital plain, its once-green awns gone gold, & now, just gone—until you reach an alpine ridge, flutter deep into the crevice of a talus, & quietly evanesce in the mountain's brokenness. When the sun loses its grip & slips behind the peak, a cloud of you arises in bacchanal, feeding on nectar of violet elephant's heads & golden mule-ears flopping in midsummer bliss, &, perhaps, on this night, abdomens touch & four wings flutter ever so briefly as a future passes to you in this darkness. One day, the mountain quakes, rocks slide, & a clawed paw crushes countless wings as it lifts them to his maw. Frantic in midday sun, you swirl light-drunk as the bear licks moth after moth from his thick brown fur until he devours all of this weather, &, perhaps, somewhere within him, you spread your wings once more, fold into yourself & disappear—

BRITTNY RAY CROWELL

a tether

my sister is shedding the virus
i imagine her from within
like a snow globe—olio of blood
and the thing that could have killed her
snowflakes sloughing sickness like skin

i think of all the men my body hosted
wonder if i'm still peeling
their touch from the inside like glue

what is the half life of bodies
tethered—how long to keep
a bird's nest left empty

imagine me grating under the grooves
of their fingers, winding
into corkscrews of ribbon
for wind to catch—for ground to settle
for grass to mend
into mingled debris
how long to purge
the imprints unseen—the damage
absorbed within me

in the stained glass of my memory
i picture peach meat under dark bark exposed
my fat bottomed heart in their palms

INDRANI SENGUPTA

catalog of failed women whom I've loved or been or prayed for

who is a robust succession of nesting dolls, identically sized, each an anagram of the others' names.

who seeds the small white arils of lexapro into her writing hand, where they may spring forth and marrow.

who revels in being meat, in being an unwrapped package of laffy taffy or whatever's the newest, most abiding metaphor. who has pawned her body for a television only to find you cannot watch television without a body.

she who loves too-small hats on too-large heads.

who is violently weaving in the portico. violently weaving in the far fringes of her own party. who invites you over, leaves out a quartet of fine french hummuses, then retires to bed so to violently weave.

for whom a bowl is a bowl is a bowl.

she who befriended her gynecologist against her gynecologist's will.

she who ministered the hawk to the hornbill, against the hornbill's will.

who is crowns of forsythia wearing a Land's End overcoat. who is gleefully smashing the wedding silver while waving across the lawn to you. yes you.

whose god gives her nothing more than she can handle and who is handling all of it and that is why she has no time for book clubs.

who is not a genus of flowering plant in the olive family. who has never even met the olive family. are they dutch? do you know them?

who stumbles and says canadia before the handsome canadian.

who is more teeth than mouth, more mouth than teeth, but never both at one time.

who is every body in the tense confrontation.

who would sooner eat the small dead hare than bury it.

the inquisitor's son

the inquisition is at a picnic, after a long day of asking questions.

you have a little schmutz on your chin, says one inquisitor to another.

but it is only rhubarb jam! they laugh. today, the inquisitors lashed

a young boy across the fingertips, then the phallus, then the fontanelle

where he was not all-yet-there, until his witch-mother keeled over

and vomited a dozen oinky black piglets onto the grass. she wasn't a

witch before but suddenly she was pulling back her tongue to reveal

a goose's serration, speaking in tongues, pulling skin from seam until

she was a five-foot mantle of horripilating fur. what wouldn't a mother do.

not like in the movies where the witch becomes a witch and it is all

vagina dentata and kittens in triquetra collars. the real witch only witches inwardly

and it is never any help at all. elsewhere, the inquisition and its wives.

one wonders how much allspice before the apple thorns. one has too

confessed to things she didn't mean for a glug of water or a half-slice of god,

but who would ask the question to that answer. one wants nothing more than

to append a many *h*'s to the end of her name, to elongate as swan neck

or as on the rack each girl becomes willower. the witch's name was alisoun, like

the middle english song. look, now an inquisitor takes his son to the far edge of the lake, holds his palm up to the solstice sky. promises silver bells

and cockleshells, where each and each and each are just extensions of the hand.

JOHN A. NIEVES

Febrile (Iteration 4)

The fever came in late   July. If the shivers were
enough to lay you down, you   were staying
down. The sick   beds may   as well
have been dirt. And you   kept taking
your own temperature, kept scratching   names
out of your address   book. On the blank   page
after *Z*, you   wrote *close your eyes and no one*
dies 'cause it's a dream. By September,   it had
burned through   and you were not   just
learning to be   an only   child, but
the only one   on the block. And maybe   now you
win every game. And maybe now   you are the captain
of every team. And when someone calls *dinner*
now, it can only mean   you. When the snow
came   to bury the graves, you   would make
footprints where the others used   to walk, then watch
the parents find the ghost   paths, hold each   other
tighter than names   with no   answers.

From Far Away

IT BEGAN WITH THE 1997 Red Valley flood. One of the largest natural disasters in North Dakota history. The levees broke near Grand Forks, flooding the area with a river the color of blood. The town disappeared underneath; houses half submerged, the rooftops like scattered steeples. The flowing landscape of orange and dark red looked like Mars from far away. People stood at the edge of their devoured towns, their eyes scanning the warped valley, searching for their homes.

Joe and I were hauling mobile homes their way. Paint chipped on the sides of our black semi, exposing the dull metal. It had no air-conditioning. There were two beds in the back, stacked like bunk beds. Joe called them *sleepers*. The cab smelled like wet clothes and the curtains separating the sleepers were thick and heavy as saddles. Things seemed like they would be okay and the farther we drove the more I believed it. It seemed to distract us from all that had happened on the farm.

Trouble pawed at me for another cheese cracker. As I held one out, he nibbled it gently, crumbs collecting in the seat. "Don't make a mess now," Joe said. Trouble was a black and tan mutt, the brown fur patches covering his paws and eyebrows, a Rottweiler and Labrador mix the man had told us. Joe named him that because he said having a dog on the road caused too much *trouble*.

We'd picked him up in Alabama. I remember waking up sweaty with hundreds of mosquito bites. Joe had already gone for breakfast inside the truck stop restaurant. I crawled out of the sleeper, popped the door open, and climbed down the side of the truck. The thick air made it hard to breathe. Walking past rows of semis, the dangerous smell of diesel hit me hard, and that's when I noticed an old man sitting on the tailgate of his beat up F150 with a dog sitting next to him. A cardboard sign between them read FREE DOG. I stopped, looked again in disbelief that someone would be giving away their dog. Trouble's head stretched high, nose twitching at all the parking lot smells, his eyes squinting in the morning sun. Someone had chopped off half of his tail, too. His owner sat there throwing hulls of boiled peanuts onto the pavement, some getting caught in his beard. He wore a Bud Light cap and dressed in more clothing than one man should for how hot it was.

I found Joe sitting down with a To Go box of eggs, grits and bacon, eating with other truckers. Joe offered me some and I scarfed it down, washing it down with a coke. "Daddy, a man outside is giving away a dog." He looked at me like I didn't need to get any ideas.

We were pulling out of the lot when Joe came to a stop.

"That dog there?" he asked.

"Yeah, that one. That man is getting rid of him. He won't have a home."

"We ain't got a home," Joe rolled his head, looking at me. "He is a good-looking dog."

Joe got out, walking over to the man. I jumped out, easing over to Trouble. He turned his head to me as I held out my hand. *He's a male*, I heard the man say. "Come here, boy," I said. The hot tailgate burned the back of my thighs as I eased down to sit with him. He came over and licked my hand. My other hand reached for his head, then down his neck and back. His hot, thick fur reminded me of a soft blanket left out to dry. He ducked his head, thrusting it up under my armpit, so that my elbow rested just along the other side of him. He turned to lick my eye. "Please," I begged Joe. "Please," I said. "I'll take good care of him."

Next thing I knew, Trouble was hopping up in our semi, me pushing his butt up the second step. He sat in my lap, paw pressed into the leather armrest, trucking along with me. He shoved his head underneath my arm as I rolled the window down, the warm wind pouring in.

Three weeks later, we were off to North Dakota. I wondered about the homes we picked up in one location, dropping off in another. They traveled hundreds and hundreds of miles on wheels, rolling on to new destinations. We'd unhitch the trailers, moving them from wheels onto cinder blocks stacked on top of the earth. New homes with kitchens and showers no human had stepped into.

We were in Chattanooga, Tennessee when Joe walked off to fill out some paperwork and I climbed up the mobile home, cracking open the door. Trouble darted in right behind me. The smell of fresh chemicals hit me first. Brand new. The soft, jungle green carpet thickened beneath my shoes like a puff of cloud. Trouble threw himself down, grunting and kicking his legs in the air. A gas fireplace sat in its stone frame, looking as if a fire were blazing behind the glass covering. The master bedroom had a huge closet with tons of cubbies for belongings. I stepped inside the large whirlpool tub. Trouble hopped in, too. I scuffed my hands all along his back, making spraying noises with my mouth. He panted, smiling at me as if thankful for the imaginary bath. I pictured my bed against the wall beneath the window, my rock collection lining the edge of the sill, and my bear lamp plugged into the outlet nearby. I could always use some light.

Three wooden bar stools lined a small bar, facing the kitchen. I recalled my mother making mashed potatoes in a mixer, the loud grinding noise that called me from the other end of the house. She used to hand me the beaters to lick off the extra potatoes. The taste of butter and salt remained on my tongue as I saw myself at the bar stool, begging for more. My mother's smile came to me, her standing beyond the fake granite counter tops. I ran my hand along the edges of the smooth stove. No sticky remains, no sign of living. The sterile smell, like a box of latex gloves, didn't remind me of home at all. Not one dirty dish or a week-old soggy sponge. The cabinets were empty except for pieces of paper and plastic and leftover sawdust. "Brooke," Joe called for me. I ran to the door, yelling back so he'd know I was in the trailer. I didn't want to continue pretending while moving 80 miles per hour down the road.

We made a stop at a Motel 8 along the way, taking a break from the heat. Trouble sat close to me, panting hard after we'd run through an open field just on the other side of the motel. The streetlights gleamed on the surface of the pool, water sloshing against the concrete edges. A mother and her son splashed and dove like dolphins playing. My feet dangled in the water as I glared up at the neon motel sign. Joe sat on the plastic poolside chairs behind me. I had no idea where we'd be the next day or the next. I watched the mother toss her son into the air. He fell into the water, disappearing for a few moments. And in the little time he disappeared, the mother's laughter filled me up with something good, and I wondered if the little boy could feel it, too, underwater, beneath the tireless night sky.

My mother said she tried to put an all-points bulletin out, but the local police refused to follow through. AMBER Alert had just been created the year before, named after the abducted and murdered 9-year-old girl from Arlington, Texas. In Georgia, they referred to it as Levi's Call. The alert named after Levi Frady, a boy who went missing, and was later found dead, and whose homicide is still unsolved. I didn't find out until later, from my grandmother, that I had been kidnapped by Joe. My grandmother drove all around Georgia looking in the parking lots of truck stops. "Lord, Brooke. You were gone a long time," she reminds me. I don't remember much as it happened so fast. That day of the gun incident when Gurley and I returned home, I watched my mother take off in her Thunderbird with my sisters. Joe taking off in his black and tan Bronco, chasing after them. How I waited and waited, until someone realized they had left me there, Gurley waiting patiently by my side. When they returned, Joe put me in the back of his Bronco as my mother fought to get me out. I didn't want to leave the farm, so I fought back. My mother left with my sisters Janie and Kim. The next day, Joe and I were gone and I didn't think anything about it.

The city lights blazed in the distance. It would be one stop of many. We must have made a hundred trips back and forth to North Dakota, carrying shelter for those who had lost so much. Joe couldn't keep a trucking partner long enough, because no one could keep up with him. He never slept, but he got Driver of the Year that year. He fell asleep at the wheel a lot, once running off the road, throwing me out of the sleeper onto the gearshift, skinning my shin from ankle to knee. I didn't sleep much after that either.

The double-wide trailers rolled along down interstate hooked to the truck, yellow tape flapping in the wind that read in huge, bold, black letters OVERSIZE LOAD. We stopped every now and then to stock up on canned Cokes and peanut butter and cheese crackers. A blue cooler filled with ice sat between our seats in the truck. For miles and miles, I heard the ice rocking against the plastic corners of the cooler and the Cokes making an orchestra of aluminum against aluminum. It sounded like half-dead fish in there trying to make it out alive.

•

A YELLOW BILLBOARD with large, bold blue writing read—*The Thing?* The scrawled question mark made it creepier. I'd seen the sign for it since El Paso and we were getting closer to Tucson. Joe thought I'd be interested in roadside attractions in the middle of nowhere.

Joe taught me how to read maps. He'd spread out the atlas, flipping the pages toward our next destination. Thousands of thin lines snaked through the landscape like veins, the blue tributaries and interstates connecting like one breathing body. The shapes of states etched in my brain, how the ragged edges of them fell off into one another. Until my eyes roamed off to the coast, where the roads ended and the world turned to a vast blue, a bright blue, not as dark as the Georgia waters back home. Joe's finger pointed to where we were, then quickly traced the map to where we were headed. He smiled, then chuckled a bit, "Now, you figure it out."

We had lived in a trailer before. A blue single-wide on Bear Lane in Funston, Georgia. I was nine months old when I almost died from copper poisoning. I swallowed a penny and it made a home in my throat for about eight weeks. I couldn't eat anything. Pepper said each time she put me to sleep on my stomach I cried and made grunting noises. She took me to the doctor but they dismissed it as some common thing babies do—refuse to eat, cry on their bellies.

Joe didn't tolerate the crying. He laid me down on pallets made of quilts and pillows as I screamed. Pepper said she kept on asking him to hand me to her so she could rock me.

"Something is wrong with that baby," she said. He refused to hand me over, saying "I'm going to learn her. She's going to listen when I tell her to stop that crying."

Joe put me in the highchair and shoved food in my mouth, food running out of one corner. Pepper told them something must be stuck in my throat. She told my mother I needed to go back to the doctor, but my mother couldn't take any more days off work. My mother worked hard, trying to raise five children.

Pepper took me to a different doctor. "I want an x-ray picture of this baby today," she demanded. The x-ray showed Abraham Lincoln sitting right there in my esophagus, the copper poisoning breeding, spilling into my bloodstream. I had a fever of 104.

The only real proof I had of our time living in that trailer was when I looked at the huge dent in the side of Joe's head. We'd gotten kicked out of the trailer because my parents couldn't pay the rent. Joe kept going back, starting trouble with the owner and some of his workers. One Saturday, Joe went back for the last time. One of the men hit him in the head with a crowbar, knocking him out cold in the front yard. My mother ran inside the trailer to use the phone and said to the men, "Don't no one care about that man in the front yard but I'm going to call 911 and if one of y'all touch me, you going to find out who loves me." My grandmother says I sat there in the stroller, watching it all happen. That was long ago, but it seemed so close to me, sitting in the truck heading down the road to nowhere. I stared at Joe. I stared at the huge oval-shaped dent in his head as if God himself left a thumbprint there, large and shiny, reminding me of the first home I lost.

Every couple of days we pulled over for showers. I had my own shower room. The key tag had a number written in black ink. The showers looked like locker rooms— tiled floor with one drain and a huge white curtain hanging from a silver rod. The lukewarm water sprayed out fast and harsh like tiny needles pricking my skin. It tasted like blood, too, a metallic tinge like rust, the kind left in your mouth after a pulled tooth.

Truckers stared at me as I came and went in and out of shower rooms. People stared at me as I walked across the wide, hot asphalt of truck stop parking lots. I didn't see any children while on the road. Not a single child. All I saw were men, hopping in and out of big trucks, their bellies full and smiles wide, wearing hats and boots, despite the summer's brutal heat. I looked forward to seeing the women who worked there. I never saw any women unless they were working at the checkout counters. The women looked at me with concern, wearing red and white aprons, jet-black mascara thickening around their eyelids, their faces wrinkled from all the Marlboro smoke breaks behind dumpsters. Sometimes they'd toss me a free peppermint as if that would cure the very thing in my life that they were curious about.

Truck stops sold all kinds of junk—old cowboy movies, postcards, walking sticks, and shot glasses advertising where we were or where we might be going next. Joe and I often ate from the buffet counters. Each time we walked into a Flying J or a Love's I could smell the fried chicken, fresh cut potato logs, and green beans. Real food that tasted like home. We'd get a couple of Styrofoam boxes, fill them up and hit the road. I'd take brochures from the counter, sometimes a local magazine. I thought they were all free until someone stopped me one day asking me to pay for it. I'd read anything I could get my hands on. As I unfolded the brochures, depending on where we were, pictures of mountains or deserts or cities popped out at me like a stand-up picture book. I'd read about white water rafting, the white curls of racing rivers splashing the sides of blow up rafts. Rattlesnakes curled beneath a cactus as a hot sunset fell down in the background. Miles and miles of hiking trails lined with trees and warnings of wildlife along the way. That summer, I believe I read every state park brochure there is in the country.

Along the spinning racks exiting the truck stops, there were stickers with pictures of lizards dressed like women. They were wearing high heels, short dresses, and red lipstick. Some had blonde hair and were leaning against trucks, smoking a cigarette. There were two types of stickers: ones that said *I Love Lot Lizards* and ones that said *No Lot Lizards Allowed*. I asked Joe what that meant because I noticed them stuck to the doors and windows of semis. He explained that lot lizards were women who came knocking on the windows of semi-trucks, trying to sleep with truckers. I learned on the road that a man's loneliness and a woman's desperation depended on one another. At the time, it wasn't a world I understood, but it was the world I was living in.

"There's a bear in the grass up ahead," Joe's driving partner called out on the CB. Slingshot was his partner's CB radio name. Joe's was Wild Bill. They warned each other of bears in the grass and alligators in the road. "Roger that," I said. Bears indicated that there were cops hiding in the medians between trees and tall grass. Alligators were the remains left behind after someone had a blowout or flat tire. It could be dangerous if you hit a piece of the tire so truck drivers liked to warn one another. As far as the bears go, well, everyone seemed to be afraid of them, except Joe, who used to be one. He was once attacked while on duty. The guy pulled a knife out, stabbed Joe in the right side, yanking the knife upwards like gutting a fish. Joe liked showing people his scar—a stab wound running from his hip all the way up to the top of his ribs. He had a scar for everything. Mostly, I aggravated Sling-Shot, asking him the same questions over and over. *Hey Sling-Shot, where we headed to now? Are you still behind us? You seen any bears or alligators up ahead in the road or in the grass?* I liked getting on the CB talking in whatever trucker lingo I had learned like, "Roger that" and "10-4." Once a trucker replied, "What's your name? Cherry Pie?" I didn't reply.

On our way to Arizona, the landscapes shifted into their own. We'd crossed an eighteen-mile-long bridge in Louisiana, snaking through the wet bottomlands of swamp and black waters. "Don't want to get stuck down there with all them gators," Joe said. My eyes leaned towards the concrete edge of the bridge, and just beyond there I saw the water. How naïve I was to its depth below us and the gravity we fought to not find out.

Before we headed to the desert, we made a trip to Tennessee. The flat, open lands gradually became rolling hills, then massive mountains, jutting out of the earth, erasing the horizon in front of us. In Tennessee, the mountains gave me a kind of comfort the oak tree gave me on the farm. The mountains seemed to be cradling me even though they were so far in the distance. I existed on that road, winding between the feet of mountains, the roots of trees tangled at the edge of highways. Joe gave me chewing gum to keep my ears from popping. At one point, I couldn't hear anything, so I stared out the window, the wind banging against my face and eyes as I watched the landscape around me, feeling the descent into valleys and back up again to the tops of mountains.

Less emptiness came with the absence of a horizon, no wide open, no question of what lay beyond. The mountains built a jagged wall around me, a barrier of hope, something I could sit inside of. I loved how we made a turn and suddenly a mountain looked so far away, how we turned a corner and the world disappeared. Then, another turn, and the mountain seemed in arm's reach—a game of joy and terror.

After Tennessee, we visited Hersheypark in Pennsylvania. The lines of parking spots were faded, almost invisible. There were cars but not as many as you would think for a water park during summertime. We were the only semi-truck parked there. I could see all the colorful water slides from the parking lot—blue, yellow, and red. A tall fence stood between us and them. Joe paid for me to get into the park, but he stayed outside. He said he'd be at the fence with Trouble watching me.

I got on the water slides closest to the fence where Joe said he'd be waiting. After going down the slide a few times, I'd forgotten about Joe and Trouble. Kids stared at me. Some asked me my name while standing in line. One kid asked me where my parents were or if I had any brothers or sisters. I watched each child go down, one by one, listening to their laughter echo down the winding, hollow tubes. I saw mothers and fathers waiting to celebrate at the bottom of slides. Water sloshed against the plastic tubes. Siblings fought over ice cream and who got to go on the next ride first. Thunder spoke from a distance and people began talking about lightening. I heard all of this. Still, I wasn't a part of the noise.

The last time I went down the slide, I rushed out of the end, landing in a shallow pool of warm water. My clothes soaked it all up like a sponge. I didn't have a swimsuit, so my jean shorts and oversized shirt clung to my skin, weighing me down. I ran over, gathering my shoes and socks. I looked up and saw Joe looking through the distance the fence put between us. He wore a green shirt, tucked inside his Wrangler jeans, with that thick, brown leather belt wrapping itself around his tall body. He had on his cowboy boots and baseball cap. He had one arm above his head, the other clinging to the fence, his giant fingers looped through the holes. He leaned into the fence until the steel wires caved.

I climbed up the truck, looking forward to seeing Trouble even though I hadn't left him very long. "What's that smell?" Joe asked as we climbed in. Trouble had gone to the bathroom in one of the sleepers. The bottom bunk, which was Joe's bed.

"That damn dog shit in my bed. I'm getting' rid of him!"

"No," I cried. "Please."

"Leaving his ass right here."

"He didn't mean to. We can't leave him."

Joe chained Trouble to the front semi tire as I cleaned up the mess. I could see why Joe was frustrated but never understood how the smell of shit outweighed the love of a dog, that someone would really want to get rid of a dog because it shit on their bed. I've read that dogs will leave us surprises in our bed out of stress or fear. Maybe Trouble didn't like living in a semi-truck. Either way, Joe finally calmed down. Trouble cowered down by the gearshift, confused from all the tension. I talked to him in a high, sweet voice, petting him along his back. Joe shifted down, his face still red as a beetroot. The semi juggled us around until we hit the smooth highway again. Trouble stood up, scrambling for my lap with his huge paws. "You want the window down, boy?" I rolled it down. Trouble's nose reached high, twitched for a second before his mouth parted into a smile, his eyes settling in the evening light.

THE *Thing?* We saw the sign again before pulling into a weigh station. The humid air settled down a bit as an evening breeze swept through the windows.

"Alright," Joe said. "Hop in the back."

"Why?"

"You ain't supposed to be with me," he said. "They don't like passengers."

The Department of Transportation kept an eye out for things like that. I jumped in the back of the cab. Joe piled blankets, clothes, and empty suitcases on top of me. It felt like a horse saddle had been thrown on my back. He pulled the black heavy curtains together as I hunched over, head in my palms, sitting on my shins and knees. Trouble stayed up front in the floorboard. He whined, pawing at the curtains. "Shh," I said.

Joe was gone forever it seemed, but I wasn't allowed to move until he got back. It got hot underneath all the covering. I used my finger to tunnel a hole through the wrinkled sheets and pants, lifting it all up just enough to peek through and breathe.

I felt the semi shift into gear and as we started moving. We sped up some more, and I knew when we hit the interstate again, the way the gears grumbled from one to the next before it became one steady sound. Joe used his fist to punch at the curtains, yelling for me to come out.

The orange glow from the truck's gauges gleamed across the dash and the headlights poured up ahead. "You'll always be my little buddy," Joe said. He grinned, cheeks puffed up to his ears, squinted eyes, teeth barely showing beneath his graying mustache. "I sure will, " I said, smiling. I watched him shift gears, one-handed, making it look effortless. His large hand curled, draping the ball on top of the shift, pushing forward and backward. His right hand was missing part of his middle finger. A horse ripped it off as he tried unloading it from a trailer. The wild horse didn't want to come out into the hands of a man. He tied a rope around the horse's neck through the rails of the trailer. Joe went to pull the horse and it hauled ass, taking his finger with him. When people asked him what happened to his finger, he'd make up a different story each time. Once, we were sitting in a steakhouse and the bartender asked about his finger. Joe told him that long ago, at some bar, a guy bet him money he wasn't a tough enough man. So, Joe said he took a beer bottle and broke it, used the glass to slice off his own finger. I slapped him on the shoulder and said, "That ain't true, a horse took it off."

Back in Georgia, I once saw an Arabian horse I wanted. He was solid black and every muscle in his body looked alive as he ran perfect circles around the ring. His body looked like a giant, shiny cluster of knotted silicon rocks. His mane hung between his eyes, long, shaggy along the forehead and ears. He'd been beaten by men who owned him in Texas. The horse hadn't let anyone get close. They said there'd be no hope for taming it. Joe walked over to the ring, but the horse stomped and snorted, tucked its head and bucked away. Calmly, I walked to the other side and put my hand through the railings. "Over here, horsey, horsey." The Arabian turned to me, throwing his hips around, kicking up dirt. He lifted his head, mist coming from his nostrils, his ears absorbing my soft words, "Come here horsey, I won't hurt you." He began to trot my way. As he got closer, I grew nervous, as he stopped at times to dig his front hooves into the dirt, cocking his head to the side, glaring at me with one large, dark eyeball. I stretched my hand out more, calling him. He came closer. He came to my hand, nudged it gently. I ran my hand from his nose up to his forehead, parting the mane between his eyes. He stared into me as if he'd been looking for me.

He made strange words with his lips. Joe came over and he bucked away again. C.L. said he must not like men very much, because I'd been the only one able to touch him.

"Can we get this one, daddy?"

"No."

"Why not?"

"If you can't tame it, there ain't no need for it."

With Joe's love for horses also came his stubbornness to tame them, even though they had the right to remain wild. Not even an animal as powerful as a horse was a match for him. He once punched a horse in the side of the head and knocked it out. All because the horse wouldn't listen to him. He believed animals belonged under the reign of men. Sometimes he'd lean over, looking me in the eye, pointing his finger, "Now, you remember this, " he said. "Someone would rather sandpaper a tiger's ass than mess with your daddy." I'd shake my head in agreement.

I climbed down the semi, the Arizona sun slapping heat against my face and neck. The mountains peaked in the distance behind a Dairy Queen attached to the museum. The building had a sign across the top identical to the billboards, except it read MYSTERY OF THE DESERT.

Joe paid a couple of bucks to get us in the cave-like entrance—a small black door leading to three sheds on the other side. I don't remember much of what we passed by in the first two. We kept following the yellow footprints painted on the walkway until we came to the third shed. It had no doors, just two openings—one way in, one way out.

There were two indistinguishable bodies, laid out in a coffin-like concrete box with a glass top. At first, the bodies looked to be made out of clay, malleable enough to be shaped into anything. Their eyes, noses, mouths blurred in a way that looked like they were slowly melting. They looked soft, but then I could tell by the thin papery arms and legs that they had hardened and had been stuck like that for a long time. They appeared to be smaller than humans. One body taller than the other, and bigger, too. The small one rested in the arms of the other, its head turned slightly away. They said it was a mummified mother and child. I wondered if that's how me and my mother would end up, her cradling my stiffened body, her vague smile crinkling beneath, our embrace displayed to tell the story of mother and daughter. I decided their bodies were nothing but gray dust, and if I lifted the glass lid enough to pucker my lips and blow, they'd disappear into the desert wind.

We still had miles and miles to go before we reached Los Angeles, the landscapes had changed drastically, winding through Texas, New Mexico, and Arizona. Wide open. Not many trees, just sand and heat moving across the road. No shelter, no protection. Emptiness began to fill my chest again as my eyes scanned the dirt horizon circling us. Traveling through its stretched-out body across miles and miles of road signs, the desert seemed to swallow me, silencing me for days. Staring at the dry openness through the window, I worried about getting stranded there and wondered how long we could survive. I longed for something familiar like the mountains in Tennessee, enveloping me in their presence.

The desolation made me panic about the way I had been feeling about the separation of my family. Without consistency, it's difficult to trust anything. I didn't know where we'd be from one day to the next. One day, Joe would tell me he wasn't my father, then laugh, saying he was only joking. He'd put a gun to his head one day, then pray not to die the next. And according to him, he didn't kidnap me. He said my mother gave me to him because the new man she was dating didn't want children. But after she gave me away the man dumped her, telling everyone he couldn't believe a woman would get rid of her kids because a man didn't want them. There's no way of knowing a truth almost as old as me.

At night, the desert temperature dropped, the hot air turning cool. The night sky was jam-packed with stars, eternal blackness taking me with it.

"Daddy, when are we going home?"

"I don't know."

"Are we going back to the farm?"

I thought about the farm back home and the oak tree that endured storm after storm without me, and Gurley, who I never told goodbye. The farm was my home, yes, *my* home and I didn't want to leave, no matter how bad things were. I didn't know any different. I didn't know any better. From far away, home was a mirage, no more real to me than a body of water was to a thirsty animal. Trouble laid across my chest in the back sleeper, his heart thumping against my chest as I fed him crackers, making a mess. I pushed the sweat from my forehead, soaking my hair as Trouble rested his eyes upon mine. I closed my eyes, feeling the roar of the semi beneath my back. Memories drifted away from me like tumbleweeds, left behind to settle where the wind abandoned them.

Translation Folio

SOPHIA DE MELLO BREYNER ANDRESEN

Translator's Introduction

Alexis Levitin

SOPHIA DE MELLO BREYNER ANDRESEN (November 6, 1919–July 2, 2004) was Portugal's foremost woman-of-letters. She won all of Portugal's poetry awards, including the prestigious Camões Prize in 1999. She also received major awards abroad, such as Italy's Petrarca Prize, France's Prix Jean Malrieu, and the Iberian Reina Sofia Award, a year before she died. Her funeral was attended by both the Prime Minister and the President of Portugal, not a likely honor for a writer here in the USA.

Sophia was best known for her poetry, infused with her love of the sea, of classical Greece, and the endless quest for justice. I began to work with her in 1977 and, over the years, published her work in close to fifty literary magazines, including *The Anglican Theological Review, Boulevard, Chelsea, The Denver Quarterly, The Literary Review, Northwest Review, Poetry International, Prairie Schooner, Puerto del Sol* and *Translation*. These translations also appeared in numerous anthologies such as *The Vintage Book of Contemporary World Poetry*, where she was the lead entry in the 600-page collection, *Women Poets of the World* (Macmillan), *Women in Literature* (Prentice-Hall), *Leading Contemporary Poets* (Poetry International), and *Gods and Mortals* (Oxford University Press).

In addition to poetry, her first love, Sophia wrote a good deal of prose. Her eight children's books remain popular, and some have gone into a 20th edition, and beyond. Her criticism includes an influential study of ancient Greek art called *The Nude in Classical Antiquity*. As for her short stories, they were collected in two volumes: *Exemplary Tales* (1962) and *Tales of Land Sea* (1984). My translation of *Exemplary Tale*s was brought out by Tagus Press in 2015. *Tales of Land and Sea* will be coming out later this year from the same publisher.

However, the two stories appearing in this issue of *Copper-Nickel* have been drawn from a slim posthumous publication, *Quatro Contos Disperso, (Four Fugitive Pieces)*, assembled by her daughter, Maria Andresen, four years after her mother's death. Those fugitive pieces had never been included in a book-length publication. The two stories appearing here were first published in Portugal's principle literary periodical, *Colóquio-Letras*, in 2002.

Sophia liked to travel by train, enjoying the "monotonous and gentle pace that leaves our thoughts free and in peace. . . ." She took special delight in the luxury of a largely empty car, giving her "space and independence." On this trip, she was looking forward to several hours of quiet reading about education in ancient Greece. But, alas, there was a couple further down the first-class wagon and they seemed disconcerted, even astonished, at encountering someone reading a book. Throughout the leisurely journey to Lisbon, the couple returned persistently to stare at the unusual phenomenon. First the man came to her compartment door and, without a salutation, said "Are you reading a book, Madam?" An hour later he returned: "Are you still reading, Madam?" A few minutes later, he returned: "Well, then, have you not stopped reading, Madam?" Perhaps an hour later the couple returned, and this time the wife accosted Sophia: "Are you actually reading, Madam?" When the train was about to arrive at its destination, the woman returned to deliver a final quizzical salvo: "Do you like reading, Madam?" And so ends this light, ironic tale about the cultural gulf that can be found in a first-class train carriage, rattling its comfortable way from the Algarve to Lisbon. Sophia's unstated social commentary is clear.

When the dictator Salazar finally lost power and his forty-eight-year dominion over Portugal was ended by the peaceful carnation revolution of April 25th, 1974, Sophia, an aristocrat who had always struggled for social and political justice, was soon elected to the Constituent Assembly by the Oporto circle of the Socialist Party. In the excitement accompanying this major political and social upheaval, she was asked to write a story about this time of enormous change. "The Blindman" is her effort at depicting the hopes and fears of many witnessing the vicissitudes of the confused first months of the revolution. At first there was utter joy, as they now lived "without doubts or shadows . . . in a state of levitation, without sleep, without hunger, never tired, feeling no weight. . . . It seemed as if evil were simply gone . . . as if life itself had returned to its true self." But then began inevitable political in-fighting and demagoguery, threatening to swallow up the revolution's ideals. On the street, the eternal blindman had replaced his tawdry song about Toulouse-Lautrec with the vibrant and fashionable "Onward, Comrade!" But Sophia and her friends, though favoring the left, feared the worst from the fanatical rhetoric of the most extreme Communist pretenders. When a Communist coup was defeated by the democratic left, they all breathed a sigh of relief and slept more soundly. And then, one morning the blindman descended the street with his concertina, having returned to his tawdry song about Toulouse-Lautrec:

> Toulouse-Lautrec
> Alas, a cripple.
> To the Moulin Rouge
> He'd go to tipple.

The song which had distressed her before, now came as a somewhat ironic affirmation of continuity. Life would, indeed, go on, and life would be better for all, perhaps even for the blindman, in this new, long-awaited democracy.

Though these two brief tales lack the deep beauty of Sophia's love of the sea, so dominant in her poetry, they do demonstrate her sure hand, her precise control of language, and her light, ironic touch. I feel a special pleasure in translating the prose of a writer who remains, essentially, a poet at heart.

The Blindman

FOR YEARS, EVERY SUNDAY, FROM behind the half-closed shades, a bit before noon, I would watch a blindman go down the street, to the sound of his concertina. Almost always his passing gave me a half hour of bad conscience. For, usually on Saturday evening we would go out and, having gone to bed at an unseemly hour, the following day, when he would be passing by, I would be beneath the tumult of the shower or, in a rush, hurriedly getting dressed while finding nothing. As a result, no matter how quickly I ran, I never managed to get down the stairs and to the front door in time to give him the money he hoped for, and which he deserved.

He played popular songs in such a way that, even if they were joyful and ani-mated, they would take on a certain nostalgic resonance, as they echoed against the thick walls that lined the streets of this old neighborhood. The further off he went, the more the sounds would descend the sidewalk with him and, only quite a while after he had turned the corner, would they totally disappear. Even inaudible, they would still leave behind them a trail of melancholy.

Until a misfortune occurred: in a certain theater in Lisbon there appeared a film with a romanticized version of the life of Toulouse-Lautrec. It was a horrid film, filled with overly obvious images and all the voyeurism and sentimentality reeking of assured ticket sales. Even worse: the film had a musical score designed to match the images and, throughout the city one could hear the song of Tou-louse-Lautrec, in its dreadful Portuguese translation:

Toulouse–Lautrec
Alas, a cripple.
To the Moulin Rouge
He'd go to tipple.

I am a person of strong aversions, and I felt a special horror for that film, that music, and that translation.

Well, on a certain Sunday, shortly after the opening of the film, while I was still asleep in the sweet penumbra of the Venetian blinds, I dreamt that I could hear that sinister song: befuddled, I awoke with a start and leapt up in bed. It wasn't a dream: it was the blindman. Very slowly he was going down the street and his concertina was wailing the fate of Toulouse-Lautrec along the walls. The cries were so piercing that, even after he had turned the corner and gone off in the distance, and one could no longer hear the sound, there still remained in the air a long trail of importunate lament.

In the beginning, I hoped it was just a passing thing. But no: it had come to stay. Sunday after Sunday, week after week, month after month, the concertina wailed its hymn of despondency.

I must admit that my sympathy for the blindman was shaken. I had grown accustomed to watching him pass, with erect stance and probing footsteps, upright and clean in his modest clothes, with his face and its blind pupils, smooth, serene, impassive—as impersonal as the face of Homer. And now, every Sunday, he went on playing that unchained lamentation.

Luckily, with the passing of time, and my sleeping late, I grew accustomed to not hearing him.

And as the years passed, we came in 1974 to the 25th of April.

At the end of long decades of a meticulous dictatorship, the sudden change led to an incredible celebration, an intense and confident joyousness, without doubts or shadows. For several days I lived in a state of levitation, without sleep, without hunger, never tired, feeling no weight. In the street everyone was smiling, no one shoved or pushed. It seemed as if evil was simply gone. Small groups of very young people rose up, crossing the city squares diagonally with a flag in front of them, running in a triangle like a flock of migratory birds. Other groups seemed a corps de ballet which, aery and light, was crossing the stage. It wasn't just politics that had changed, it seemed to us as if life itself had returned to its true self. It seemed to us that the dream of Rimbaud had been fulfilled and that poetry had become something within daily life.

On the Sunday following the 25th of April, in spite of having gone to bed late, I got up early. Towards noon, I was talking on the phone, when I heard far off on the street a concertina playing the song "Onward, Comrade!" I ended my conversation and as fast as possible ran to the window. The blindman had already come to the bottom of the street. But his music echoed strongly from the walls and filled the street completely with enthusiasm and proclamation. I laughed with joy. What was happening out there was much more important than ideologies: the blindman had put aside his lamentations, was affirming and proclaiming his dream, his hope, his confidence.

Sometime later, I found myself with one of my friends, a lovely, generous woman of the far left. She was still utterly intoxicated by the celebration. Together we talked non-stop and laughed with joy. Suddenly, she grew silent for a moment, turned serious, and said: "Even if one day it all turns out badly, at least there were these days in which we had all this."

But those days were relatively short-lived. At the end of a few months, things began to deteriorate. Slowly the celebration was disappearing, eaten up by demagoguery, opportunism, fanaticisms, real or assumed, and various, confusing episodes in the struggle for power. Vociferating minorities of diverse creeds occupied without break the front of the stage.

In all this there was simultaneously something threatening and something unreal.

Meanwhile, every Sunday, the blindman would go down the street playing "Onward, Comrade!" Although at that time the aggressive and a bit mysterious fanaticism of the Communist Party both irritated and intrigued me, the song of the blindman never irritated me. I expected that he would continue to play it Sunday after Sunday.

Meanwhile, on the streets, on the radio, in the newspapers, on television, in speeches and in actions, demagoguery was growing unseemly and almost omnipresent, corrupting language. I began to think back to the phrase from Heraclitus: "The worst of all disasters would be the death of the word."

Many approved with enthusiasm the rhetoric of the demagogues. But, through the confusion, here and there, voices arose defending another understanding of liberty. And here and there popular intelligence cocked its ear.

On television, one day, there appeared a journalist giving a report from the north of the country. On the screen one could see a tall peasant, thin and silent, climbing with large and deliberate steps a steep hillside, while the journalist with microphone in hand, ran after him. Finally, he managed to catch up and he asked him:

"What do you think of the 25th of April?"

"Of what year?" responded the peasant.

And stoically he continued on his way.

The majority of people feared extremes and disapproved of excess. Therefore, when the Socialist Party called its supporters to the streets, a large portion of the population joined them, in immense and orderly demonstrations that grew by the day.

But during those long months, in the cold of winter, the winds of springtime, or the heat of summer, the blindman, every Sunday, at the same time, would pass through the neighborhood and, slowly, go down my street playing "Onward, Comrade!" I suppose that even the most reactionary of godmothers in the neighborhood who, through the crack of a misaligned window, with sharpened eye and alert ear, kept watch over everything happening on the street, would smile to hear him, touched by the joy of his state of grace.

Meanwhile, the Revolutionary Period followed its course: demonstrations and counter-demonstrations, coups, conspiracies, dreams, projects, illusions and disillusionment. And instability continued: no one knew what coup, what conspiracy, what new path would come next.

Finally, on a certain night in November, just before dinner, two disturbing personages appeared on the television screen. One of them had a closed, fanatical face and said nothing. The other had a fanatical, sharp-featured face, and he told us that finally everything would change: a coup from the extreme left had taken over.

My spirits sank to my feet: I didn't want to be governed by fanatics. No matter what.

The said personage continued to present the news in a peremptory tone of voice that must have frightened more than half the country: he seemed an inquisitor—that was how I imagined the obsessed fixed stare of the inquisitors. But at a certain moment, he hesitated. Someone we could not see must have given him a sign. Something had happened. Then, the person with the sharp face, maintaining with an icy line his impassivity, told us that he had to interrupt the broadcast, but that it would soon continue.

The screen went blank and soon after an old Danny Kaye film came on.

The following day, we discovered through the newspapers that there had been a coup by the "fundamentalist left," but that it had been defeated and the democratic left had taken control of the situation. I breathed a sigh of relief, and, on Saturday night, talked with various friends until very late. We all agreed that now, under a democratic peace, it was necessary to pay attention to concrete, real problems of people and of the country and put aside political games. I went to bed in the early hours, and in spite of it all I slept soundly.

The following day I slept late. But in the golden penumbra of a Sunday of wintry sun, I awoke with a start. It was the blindman.

Slowly, with probing steps, he was descending the street, while his concertina wailed along the thick walls of our old part of town:

Toulouse-Lautrec
Alas, a cripple.
To the Moulin Rouge
He'd go to tipple.

Reading on the Train

THAT SEPTEMBER, I LET THE family head back to Lisbon without me, while I stayed alone at the beach to enjoy the last days of summer.

Until the waters of the sea grew chill and nights on the balcony began to shiver beneath the wild buffeting of the wind. Then I decided that the time had come for me to leave.

I also decided to go home by train.

For the train seems to me much better than the road, with its curves to one side then the other, its long lines of buses, all that passing, cars out of their lane, the violence and impatient intensity of the rush. And the old trains go along at a monotonous and gentle pace that leaves our thoughts free and in peace—especially if we have the fortune to be travelling in a half-empty car.

So, on the day of my departure, when I arrived at the station, I thought that destiny was on my side. In fact, there were many passengers, but all of them were tourists with packs on their backs, piling into the numerous second-class carriages. The only first-class carriage was practically empty. There were only two passengers there, both seated right near the door, in the first compartment: it was a couple, husband and wife, seated face to face and turned toward the corridor, obviously watching to see who was coming in. After them, various empty compartments. I installed myself in the last one, delighted with the comfort that comes from space and independence.

The train began to move, and I closed the window beside me, but left the door wide open to the corridor, with its numerous windows through which a continual, healthy flow of air was blowing. As long as we followed the coast, I remained gazing at the distant glistening of the sea and, closer by, the nostalgic 19th century stations with their leafy magnolia trees. When the train turned towards the interior, I settled in, took from my beach bag an excellent little book on education in ancient Greece, and began to read. There was a comfort and a special restfulness in the emptiness of the compartment, and I was happy in the thought that around three hours of reading lay before me, "without any disturbances, phone calls, visits, or the usual quotidian problems. In fact, for more than an hour I read almost without stopping, interrupted only by the brief and discrete appearance of the conductor and a few pauses here and there to ponder what I was reading, gazing out the window at passing rows of trees, hills, and fields.

And then someone walked down the corridor and, looking askance, I recognized the man I had seen close to the entrance in the first compartment. He passed by two times and then, the third time, he stopped in front of my door. I lifted my head for a moment and saw that he was staring at me in great astonishment. I became somewhat astonished, as well, but luckily, a few moments later, he walked away and went to the other end of the corridor. I felt him returning and stopping once again at my door, but I didn't lift my head, although he waited there a while. Then he made another trip slowly to the end of the corridor, but came back again and once again stopped in the same place. I changed my position, turned toward the window with my back towards the door, and thought: "Could there be something unusual about this compartment? Could I be standing on my head?"

When he finally returned to his place, I looked at myself in the mirror and examined the things around me. I didn't find anything unusual, anything strange that could have drawn his interest. I began to read again, but after half an hour I heard his footsteps again and, once again, he stopped in front of my compartment, mulling over who knows what thoughts. I did not lift my head from my book and after a few minutes he went away.

I felt he wouldn't come back, and for a long time I went on reading and thinking in peace.

But then I heard again the hesitant and heavy tread that would stop for a moment in front of my door and then continue on, going from here to there, until it came to a stop in the same spot. I turned slowly towards the window and immersed myself in the book, but he gave a little cough to draw my attention and took a step forward into the compartment.

I was forced to look up. He had a perplexed and worried look. I wondered: "What could this be all about?" And I said:

"Good afternoon."

He asked:

"Are you reading a book, Madam?"

"I am," I answered.

And I turned to my book again.

My visitor went away. I took a deep breath and, once again, hoped with that clarification that he wouldn't come back to visit me again.

However, after another thirty or forty minutes, here he was again. When I sensed him coming, I turned to the window so my back was to the door. But it was hopeless. He took a step into the compartment and gave a little cough to announce his presence. I turned and stared at him without saying a word. A bit disconcerted, he hurriedly asked:

"Are you still reading, Madam?"

"I am," I replied.

He turned around and returned to his compartment. I took a deep breath.

I went on reading since the book was excellent, but after four or five pages I heard his footsteps once again. He was coming slowly, as if he wanted to pass by unnoticed. He spent some time going back and forth, but he came to a halt in the usual place.

When I finally lifted my head, he smiled and asked:

"Well, then, have you not stopped reading, Madam?"

"No," I answered.

He gazed at me with a disoriented look and disappeared.

When I was alone, I closed my eyes for a few minutes.

After that, I checked the time on my watch and opened the window in order to breathe in the smell of the fields. But I quickly closed it, since it created a draft with the open door. I refreshed my make-up in the compartment mirror. I sat down again and returned to my book.

For a long time, no one appeared, then night began to fall. The lights in the car came on.

At a certain point, the train accelerated and began to rock. After a few minutes, I could hear two people coming down the corridor. As they passed, I could see that it was the same man. Now he had his wife with him. They went up and down the corridor, passing my door in silence. After passing by a number of times, they stopped and the woman took a step into my compartment.

I raised my head and furrowed my brow. But the woman, refusing to be intimidated, asked:

" Are you actually reading, madam?"

"I am," I answered.

And I gazed intently into my book once again.

They moved away, whispering to each other.

I looked at my watch; we would be arriving in three quarters of an hour. The train swayed, panted, and whistled, as if tired of the journey. With the bad light and the swaying, reading became difficult. In the darkness, illuminated stations went flying by.

Time went on passing and the couple did not appear again.

But then they did. Jostled by the rocking of the train, the two of them came down the corridor. Hearing them coming, I picked up my book and held it so as to cover my face. However, without any more hesitations, detours, or delays, they stopped in front of my door and came into my compartment. The woman addressed me:

"Madam."

I lifted my head and replied:

"Yes?"

"Do you like reading, Madam?"

"I do."

The train began a long, final whistle.

We're about to arrive," the man exclaimed. "We have to go."
And off they went, the two of them, in a great rush down the corridor.

Translated from the Portuguese by Alexis Levitin

ADA LIMÓN

A Good Story

Some days—dishes piled in the sink, books littering the coffee table—
are harder than others. Today, my head is packed with cockroaches,

dizziness and everywhere it hurts. Venom in the jaw, behind the eyes,
between the blades. Still, the dog is snoring on my right, the cat, on my left.

Outside, all those redbuds are just getting good. I tell a friend, *The body
is so body*. And she nods. I used to like the darkest stories, the bleak

snippets someone would toss out about just how bad it could get.
My stepfather told me a story about when he lived on the streets as a kid,

how he'd, some nights, sleep under the grill at a fast food restaurant until
both he and his buddy got fired. I used to like that story for some reason,

something in me that believed in overcoming. But right now all I want
is a story about human kindness, the way once when I couldn't stop

crying because I was fifteen and heartbroken, he came in and made
me eat a small pizza he'd cut up into tiny bites until the tears stopped.

Maybe I was just hungry, I said. And he nodded, holding out the last piece.

ROME HERNÁNDEZ MORGAN

Dream in Nuclear Imaging

What does it mean
to say *left over* . . .
to say *remains*?
Like the edges of blanket
the nurse tucks
beneath my arms and legs
as I lay upon the table.
Lo que sobra:
something so abundant
it couldn't be used in time
and thus became unnecessary.
An extra plate at the table.
Rice left in the pot.
Some springs never run dry.
But these bodies—the sun
drags away what it wants
leaving only salt
on our brown shoulders.
What remains of us?
A surgical wound.
You, waiting worried
in my hospital room.
How exhausting, holding still,
keeping everything in place.
Pinned down, I dream
I lift my arm to offer you
a glass of water.

PAUL GUEST

What I Believe

Last night my mouth filled with blood
and I had been falling forever
in the darkness. Down the street
an old skating rink burned
up. There was lightning and fire
and a bored crowd
and a school bus speeding into the distance.

Where: the chalk shadow
of near-by mountains
and in the wet air the metallic plunk
of banjos. Everything
is too fast, just now.

Birds drop from ratty nests
in a dream
that is unsettling years later:
a peacock coughing,
blue-green feathers lousy with plague.

Forgive me. I'm scared
of the news. That Australia is aflame
and may be dead before
up-jumped real estate magnates from Queens.

My legs hurt. A molar
on the left side of my mouth
sings like I'll care, soon enough.
That I'll heal. Love,
do you have change for a jukebox
that exists inside
the sick tide of fever
and is filled entirely with old country songs?

Despair in its way
can be quaint
when there are no ashes in the wind.
When the water
isn't thick with lead
and this reference isn't punishingly obvious.

NICK LANTZ

The Waffle House Index

—an informal metric used by FEMA to gauge disaster severity

In ancient Babylon, they tied three answers to three arrows,
and whichever flew farthest told the truth. Today, I shopped
online for face masks for my cats. If Waffle House stays open,
will the armed gunmen parading the capitol fly away like angry
birds? Will the medieval muck serfs walked in stop sticking
to our shoes? Will the wheelbarrow of dead bodies cease
its rattle? The word "we" makes a crooked sound when we
talk disaster, but please recognize that every apocalypse requires
its own measure of ruin. Ours just happens to be pan-fried.
Others read dust, placenta, barley, the melting of wax, needles,
cracks in a burning donkey's skull, comet tails, even—don't laugh—
poetry. The trick is, you only get a stone's answer from a stone.
You shuffled the deck. You ordered hash browns ALL THE WAY.
To the executioner, the word *hope* just sounds like *rope*.

ALICIA MOUNTAIN

Manhattan, OK

September in Oklahoma, when rain comes down like it got permission.
A loose underpart of my hatchback holds on and continues to worry me.
I have a job, but it feels like I don't, but not in a vacation way.
I have a body and a girlfriend, books to write, to read, and no dog.
Some of this will stay the same when the rest changes, or vice versa.
September somewhere else with different bumper stickers on trucks.
September the year we get permission to love or stop waiting for it.
The friends of mine whose love I trust the most are unimpressed.
Alex at an east side bar a year ago, elaborate cocktails with smoke and crystal.
I was on a treadmill and told him I'd be there in an hour, didn't shower.
Unimpressed by any machine, unimpressed by anyone trying to impress.
At the drive thru testing site they stick my vial under my windshield wiper.
I have a body and a car and both should get some diagnostic attention.
Rain while I'm idling in a parking lot, rain like any city in its melancholy.

Adages for Dragons

I am still living in the newly democratized Czechoslovakia. Coming home I stab the shoehorn where the sting meets the fat bottom lip of my shoes. I tower over them, slayed, the tongues out. My shoes lie on their sewn leather cheeks all night. It is a street named for the puppet master and his dragons beloved by children. It takes time for a well-meaning notion to die. All broken appliances date back to communism. The puppeteer died of dubious causes. The flat is hot and narrow. The roller windows do not budge. No age fully ushers out another. And I lie sheetless, sweaty, dreaming of my shoes: two heads of a smoldering body, wheezing in its barrow.

COREY VAN LANDINGHAM

Reader, I

made my mother cry. Basement of the Italian café, candles cascading over themselves with wax. A wan Chianti to celebrate thirty-three. We had always shared our plates (had the same tongue, same taste for citrus and pâté), but I ordered the whole branzino for myself. It was always known that I would wait, but now—would it break her heart, I asked? The wavering chin. The hard glance away. She could have taken a few more seconds before the Yes. I picked at the hem of my birthday dress. It was getting late. Couples migrated to the same side of dark booths. Our waiter asked—her napkin hadn't even made it to her lap—if everything was okay? Her only chance, no steadfast sibling to take the heat. Was I sure? She had me at forty, and of course it was a change and yes the nights were long and bodies start to weigh, to sag regardless. I think you'll . . . I wouldn't. Her squid ink cavatelli began to stink. I wanted to fill myself with something else—hollow-stemmed coupes of Champagne, shade-grown coffee, beef tartare alone at noon. We could take that trip to Saint-Tropez! If, if he did leave, I'd be fine. I looked down into my wine. We hadn't yet decided. The issue had been raised. But I need long runs along a country road to keep me sane. As it is, I cannot coax myself to sleep most nights, and we don't even—What I couldn't say: they'd barely get to know her, and dad would be a man we'd tell them lived once. Plus I have so little will most days to stay alive myself. And so she wept. I paid.

CATE LYCURGUS

The Giving

We were gifted. We were spendthrift and slightly adrift through the current, the present we untangled, endless as kelp, we raised up its bulbs, their buoyancy crushed, but thought we were helping, since we had been gifted: unbridled light or an overtime win; floor boards flush with gas, unclutching; the road-brushing bend of coastal acacia, their gold film a pixie dust brimming our eyes; were given dogs lifting their sweet scolded faces; steel bridges as bracelets studding the water; our waterway veins raised up through our arms; were lavished with dancing, the sock hop that started, refusing to stop, till sweaty on carpet, we fell, and we melted as butter asunder; were given surrender of into each other; were gifted slight hands, so we threw makeshift spirals; strung cartwheels through aisles; and then in our sidelot plotted with weeds, we learned how to volunteer, how to maintain; our gift was repair we were given thick voices from back pews of teeth; we thought we could give back the loose side of lightning, could retract its fracture; rubbed salve where it punctured pre- and post-given—post-rain, in stillness; post-lager, with foam. Post-frozen, we gasped through dark walnuts of lungs, wanted to offer their toasted aroma, but could not, not lift up our tangle-charmed limbs, till warmth of a doorway, of one not our own, cracked open our chests. Ushered us, guests. Unlocked the locks on our possible selves.

ABDUL ALI

This Tiny Utopia Nestled in the Archive

What I remember most are the lawns,
lines the mowers made on the deepest greenery.
The sparse trees that lined the neighborhood.
Remember the peach tree in the backyard?
The modest semi-detached homes filled with
people that looked, spoke, and drove Buicks like us.
The airplanes that flew over our roof daily
on their way to LaGuardia Airport
The green-and-white lawn chairs—
That made tic-tac-toe boxes on my legs
& me counting the clouds—
which I mistook for fat-assed sheep.
The extravagant Sunday church hats
That moved like ceiling fans.
The holiday parties & basement parties.
The slow drag. The red bulbs replacing the white.
And in general, feeling like a silhouette peeling
from yourself. Stuck in the background wanting
to move center on the dance floor.
Watch me get down.

Translation Folio

SANDRA SANTANA

Translator's Introduction

Geoffrey Brock

IN THE FALL OF 2017, during a residency at the Casa del Traductor in Spain, a fellow translator told me about the book she was translating into German. She described it as a sequence of short prose poems with long titles that often related only obliquely to the body texts, but that counterbalanced or counterpointed them in surprising ways. Intrigued, I asked to borrow the volume, which turned out to be a beautifully designed chapbook called *Y PUM! un tiro al pajarito* (*And BANG! Someone Shot at the Bird*) by the contemporary Spanish poet Sandra Santana. I became even more intrigued after reading some of the poems, and before I returned it to its owner I scanned the whole thing into my phone, filing it away for future reference.

The resulting PDF lay dormant until early November of 2020, when, desperate for some distraction from election doomscrolling, I dusted it off on a whim and started trying to see how those idiosyncratic dual texts might work in English. Somehow, they proved an excellent anxiolytic, and between the election and the insurrection I eked out versions of all thirty-one of the short pieces that make up the chapbook.

I loved, first of all, how they looked on the page. The contrasting weights and textures of their double slab construction—heavy titles with bold capital letters and ragged right margins sitting squarely on top of lighter, neatly justified, lower-case bodies—created an appealing visual tension, like little monochrome Rothkos. And then, once inside the poems, I was struck by how quickly they manage to lure us into their brief mysterious dramas, thanks to what one of the poems calls "the ambiguous seduction of signs." As a reader, I often find the semantic fields of these poems slippery and my interpretive footing uncertain, but I'm also dazzled by their flashes of arresting imagery, their cerebral muscularity, and their delightful playfulness.

The chapbook's two epigraphs—"The poem traces a world that does not exist" (Ernesto Carrión) and "Come, give me your hand / What hand?" (Juan Eduardo Cirlot)—hint at the book's thematic concerns. Both evoke radical absences, and Santana herself has described the volume as "a book of exercises for thinking about absence . . . about those absences that we fill with imagination, that we fill with fantasy. It might be the absence of desire, the absence of the beloved, or the absence of the word itself." And if we understand "spiritual" in a metaphysical rather than religious sense, we might call the book, then, a series of spiritual exercises, and indeed Ignatius of Loyola's famous *Exercitia Spiritualia* seems to serve as a kind of structural model: his book is divided into four parts, each containing a week's worth of exercises; Santana's book, too, consists of four parts, the first three containing seven verbal Rothkos, the last one six.

Ben Van Wyke, who translated Santana's first book into English before his untimely death in 2017, suggests a more modern lens, describing her earlier work in terms that seem equally apt here:

> These poems resonate well with some of the fundamental notions of language in contemporary philosophy, and provide an interesting site for reflecting on these ideas, though this is not to say that they must be read through the lenses of this type of theory . . . [T]hey can be read in any number of ways, and, in fact, demand this multiplicity of readings, demonstrating their own need to be created and appropriated by readers who will, in turn, give them expression, a need which also makes them perfect candidates for translation.

This emphasis on a "multiplicity of readings" dovetails nicely with Santana's view of her own three-pronged career as philosophy professor, writer, and translator. She notes that those pursuits all share a common foundation in reading, and that reading, for her, in each of those contexts, involves "a search for an always precarious and always provisional understanding of the world." The poems in *And BANG! Someone Shot at the Bird* invite us to become provisional readers and to share in that precarious search.

•

SANTANA IS THE author of four books of poems: *Marcha por el desierto* ("Desert march," Pregunta Ediciones, 2004/2020), *Es el verbo tan frágil* ("Is the verb so fragile," Pre-Textos, 2008), *Y ¡PUM! un tiro al pajarito* (*And BANG! Someone Shot at the Bird*, Arrebato, 2014), and *La parte blanda* ("The soft part," Pre-Textos, in press). Her books have been translated into English, French, and Russian, and her poems have appeared in magazines and anthologies around the world, including Forrest Gander's *Panic Cure: Poetry from Spain for the 21st Century* (Shearsman, 2013, UK; Otis Books, 2014, US).

She is also the author of two critical volumes: *El laberinto de la palabra: Karl Kraus en la Viena de fin de siglo* ("The labyrinth of the word: Karl Kraus in turn-of-the-century Vienna," Acantilado, 2011), for which she received the City of Barcelona Essay Prize, and *La escritura por venir. Ensayos sobre arte y literatura en los siglos XX y XXI* ("Writing to come: essays on art and literature of the 20th and 21st centuries," Pregunta Ediciones, 2021). Her translations include books by Ernst Jandl (*Si no puede hacer nada por su cabeza, al menos arréglese la gorra* ["If you can't do anything about your head, at least fix your hat"], Arrebato, 2019), Karl Kraus (*Palabras en versos* ["Words in verse"], Pre-textos, 2005) and Peter Handke (*Vivir sin poesía* ["To live without poetry"], Bartleby Editores, 2009), and others. She currently teaches Aesthetics and Theory of Art at the University of La Laguna on Tenerife.

Blancaflor Hiked Up Her Skirt and Showed Them Her Secret: "Beauty Is Ever-Present, but Only for the Fearless Who Can Find Their Bearings in the Dark of Their Domains"

> What, tonight, was chance?
> Thomas Pynchon

Do circles close or open? Look carefully: it's here—in this obscene game of analogies, in the ambiguous seduction of signs—that the blah-blah-blah of the world resides.

Typology of the Invisible Straps That Fetter the Wrists and Ankles of Those Who Walk Around in Sandals and Light Dresses Unaware of Being Part of a Composition

Had she recognized earlier any violence in that minimal pressure on the skin that left no mark, she would have freed herself of it. As from the sandals lying now on the rug, next to the architect's table.

Children That We Are of Ulysses, Who Prided Himself on Being Able to Reap with a Good Sickle More Wheat Than Anyone Over a Long Day Without Eating from Dawn to Dusk

There was a point where a bird (in the sky), a train (along its tracks, under the bridge), and a car (on the road ahead) could be seen emphatically crossing paths. She felt a certain relief at moving forward while each element continued on its way and abandoned her (having stretched the briefest instant to infinity by coinciding), sensing that at any moment the encounter could happen again.

He Was Gone, and Yet the Air Was Still Stirring in the Empty Space His Form Had Left

Her finger neared the metallic surface of the door phone. This gesture would grant her a certain momentary power over the object of her desire, who, on hearing the buzzer, would reflexively drop everything he was doing to go to the door and speak to her through the intercom.

The Art of Producing Seemingly Wonderful and Unexplainable Phenomena: Escapism, Disappearances, Unions, Separations of What Remains United, Transformations, Mind Readings, Time Jumps, Etc.

Gigantic airplanes suddenly become tiny and impose—from their absurd speck-perches in the sky—immense distances. Stewardesses, with invisible gestures, make luggage vanish behind curtains; they offer passage to places built from the blurred and flickering materials of the imagination to those who just a moment ago were sitting here, beside us, observing the shifting spectacle of the concourse.

Translated from the Spanish by Geoffrey Brock

Varieties of Short Fiction

I HAVE IDEAS. I CAN'T help it.

I used to have a job where having ideas was a good thing. Or, at least, it didn't hurt.

I was a writing teacher. I was a professor, in fact, and I was often in situations, like the classes I taught, where I had to *profess*—to say interesting and maybe even helpful things about the subject matter of the class I was teaching. Like short fiction.

I'm not a teacher anymore. I quit.

But I still have ideas about short stories. Some of them come from my teaching days, others are new, and they might all be bad ideas, I'm not sure.

I've talked about them, but I haven't written them down. And I feel like you can't tell if certain things are dumb or smart unless or until you write them down.

And so.

•

SHORT STORIES, ON the whole, can be separated into two categories: those that are about *characters* and those that are about *situations*.

I know. Yes. All short stories, pretty much, feature a situation and at least one character. Without those things, it's hard to imagine you could have a short story at all.

By "situation," I mean exactly what it sounds like, the predicament a character is put in. It's the series of swimming pools arrayed across a neighborhood's back-yards. It's the brother who insists on pursuing the potentially hazardous life of a jazz musician. It's the blind man who comes over and wants to draw a building.

I'm sure there are short stories out there that don't have either a character or situation in them, but I haven't read them. If they don't exist yet, someone should write one.

But although short stories always or nearly always feature both characters and situations, it's been clearer to me, the more time I've spent reading them, that some short stories lean harder against the characters they portray than others, while others lean for support against the situations they put those characters in. I'm convinced you can draw a neat line between the stories that do one thing and the ones that do the other.

It's a question of where a story gets its momentum. It's about where the author put the engine that drives the whole thing forward.

Take "The Library of Babel" by Jorge Luis Borges.

In that story, a narrator describes in detail an impossibly vast and elaborate library whose architecture is baffling and sometimes treacherous. And while there is a narrator who speaks to us, he is not nearly as important as the situation Borges places him in, so that he can describe it. The situation, in the case of this story, is the unlikely existence of the library itself, which the narrator contemplates at some length.

The narrator, of course, is necessary to the story. Without him you don't have a story.

But it's easy to imagine switching out the narrator Borges gives us for a different character and not having the story change much. The tone might shift, inflections might modulate—and those things can matter—but at its fundamental level, the story would be more or less the same. This story is not about the character, it's about the situation the character is faced with.

Now, contrast "The Library of Babel" with "The Man Who Was Almost a Man" by Richard Wright.

That story definitely has a situation: a boy lives in poverty on a farm where he has access to a catalog through which he can buy a gun. He is convinced that acquiring a gun is his direct path to manhood.

Without that situation, you don't have a story. But the situation is not what decides the story's pivots and maneuvers, the complex machinery that the word "plot" hardly does justice to.

What does decide how those things go is the story's protagonist, the man who is almost a man, who wants so badly to grow up, and who brings calamity down on his head and his father's head in the process of trying to do it. You could take that same protagonist, place him in another situation, and expect to come out with roughly the same story.

Rather than having him live on a farm and kill a mule that someone then has to pay off for the rest of his life, you might make him a twenty-first century teenager who, by climbing a rock or something, to impress everyone and show them how strong and grown he is, gets himself injured and incurs crushing medical debt. You could have him obsess over something he sees on Amazon.com that he thinks, by having it, will mean he's grown up, when in fact it will ruin everything.

That is is partly what I think Wright's story is about, incidentally: the corrosive and potentially cataclysmic potential of the kind of desire that results from having consumer goods dangled before us, just out of reach. It used to be catalogs, now it's Amazon.

The story would change dramatically, if you reset it and changed the situation. It wouldn't be as good, but the shape of it would look much the same. You could trace its movements in the air, and it would look much like the movements of the original.

That short story is led by its character, and not by its situation.

•

I'LL BE THE first to say it: this situation vs. character distinction in short fiction may be one of those things that's fun to talk about in school but doesn't look like much when you put it on paper.

I'm okay with that. I have had fun in my life, and it's all been worth it. I am relatively happy 12 percent of the time, and that's an all-time high.

But I've found this character/situation thing can be helpful in two ways. The first is that it helped some students, when I was teaching their classes, get interested in short fiction.

The distinction I'm describing here is an easy one to make; you can make it based on simple observations. One way to start a conversation with students about a short story is to ask them, "Is this story primarily about its characters, or is it about the situation it puts them in?" You have to explain what you mean, but in order to answer the question students have to delve into the story, to refer to different aspects of it in order to make their case.

Once they do that, they've begun to walk the path of close-reading. They are on their way.

It's also helpful because most of the younger students have been living for years on a diet of Marvel, Disney, and video games. And as much as I enjoy those things, they don't prepare you for "Paul's Case" by Willa Cather, which is about a young, queer man who leaves home for the city and steals money on the way so he can enjoy the luxury he is convinced he ought to have been living in all his life. It's a story that takes its time, and not everyone is used to that. Explaining to students that some but not all short stories privilege characters over situations, and that this is one of those stories, can help prevent younger students from giving up on the genre because they think it's boring. And that's something I tried to prevent from happening as a writing teacher. I considered it to be part of my job.

But the character/situation distinction is useful to me, too, as a writer of short stories.

It's not something I think about when I *start* writing a story. But it often happens that I get to some approximate midpoint of a story's composition and find I'd have an easier time removing the fingernails of my own left hand than it would be to figure out what in the world I'm even trying to do with the story and where it's going.

It happens the same way every time, and I never see it coming. I have a strong idea of what the story is when I start writing it, but I lose my way somewhere.

And while that is a sure sign the story is coming to life, that it's turning out to be more than I expected, that it's straining against the leash I put on it because it knows there's a better destination than where I'm trying to go—it's right over there! just *look!*—it makes me feel, every time, like I am the dumbest loser on the planet, and that I should have gone to law school years ago when that was still an option.

I mean, when an engineer designs a bridge, they don't feel good when it turns out that what they were planning all along was really a dam. They lose their job if they do that.

Throughout my writing life, I've been learning to feel more at home in moments like the one I'm describing, to see those rough patches not as problems to be surmounted but the very point of writing, the reason it's worth doing in the first place. You're supposed to have the rug pulled out from under you; you're supposed to have to rethink what you're writing a hundred times on the way to completing it.

Writers don't do their work because it's easy. They do it because it's one of the hardest things anyone can do, and they're the only ones who have a chance at doing it right. Right?

Anyway. This character/situation distinction can be useful in those confounding moments, when you're lost and don't even know anymore, if you ever did, what you're trying to do when you get this stuff on paper. I have found it helpful to step back and ask if I'm writing a character story or a situation story. It can clarify the work ahead, casting a new light on it so I can get the work done.

It doesn't make the job easy. It's still incredibly hard, and it drives me nuts.

Sometimes when I am writing a story, I think I am the worst person for the job. Sometimes I want to walk into the woods and disappear.

•

I HAD A grad student, years back, when I still had students, who was great, but who insisted that the character/situation split I chose to see in short fiction was a way to project a masculine/feminine divide onto the genre.

She thought female writers wrote character stories, while men wrote about situations—or, rather, that this impression was the unfortunate outcome of looking at short fiction through this prism. The prism was flawed, and it led to a flawed conclusion.

But I never believed that. I always disagreed.

I don't think she was wrong to be suspicious of the practice. It's always pretty dodgy to divide things, art included (or especially), into separate categories. As helpful as the character/situation distinction has been for me, as a writer and as a teacher, the utility of such a thing is bound to have limits.

But the character/situation split is not a veiled attempt to ascribe genders to different short stories. There's nothing masculine nor feminine about a short story. And it's way too easy to give examples of women-identified writers who wrote primarily about situations, and male-identified writers who wrote mostly about characters.

Shirley Jackson's "The Lottery," like many of her short stories, is about a situation. It's what the whole story is concerned with. The characters in it aren't given much depth, and their lives beyond what's on the page aren't important. What's important is the situation they find themselves in, which the reader doesn't fully understand until the story's brilliant and horrifying end.

"A Good Man Is Hard to Find" is about a situation: a bunch of people from the same family who despise each other have to ride in the same car. The grandmother's interior life is important to the story; it's her vague and fickle memory, dredged up from a shallow and hateful inner life, that redirects them to that roadside where the family is wiped out by the Misfit. But it's the situation that matters most. It's the family's getting stuck in the car together that decides the direction of the story.

And the studs of the world that we call "guys" or "men" write character-oriented stories all the time. "Sonny's Blues," by James Baldwin, has a prominent situation—a man's brother embraces a life the narrator frowns on, and gets in trouble with heroin and the law—but the character of the narrator, and of the brother, are of supreme importance to the story. Character is the engine that drives that particular masterpiece.

·

In order to belabor the thing I'm going on about in this essay, I'll refer to two texts from the nineteenth century, one of which is about characters, the other of which is about a situation.

I've chosen these stories because I like them, and because they're old enough that I can quote from them heavily without getting into a dicey copyright situation.

"The Yellow Wallpaper," by Charlotte Perkins Gilman, starts with its narrator establishing her current situation. She is, we learn, married to a man named John. We know they're not so rich, because she says they don't often get to stay in houses like the one they're staying in for the duration of the story.

John is an asshole. "John is practical in the extreme," the narrator tells us. "He has no patience with faith, an intense horror of superstition, and he scoffs openly at any talk of things not to be felt and seen and put down in figures." He is "a physician," and she admits outright that his being a physician is probably why she hasn't been recovering from her present affliction. "You see," she writes, "he does not believe that I am sick!"

I will never tire of "The Yellow Wallpaper."

It is a perfect short story. It is the most fun short story to teach that I ever taught—students, I found, always, when I had students, fucking loved it.

It is utterly of its time (1892) and yet feels like something current, like something someone would write today about the state of things in 1892. And it had a purpose.

As the author herself explained later, in an essay on "The Yellow Wallpaper," she based the story on the traumatizing isolation treatment she was given, for what today we'd call postpartum depression. She had to lie in bed and not read or write or do anything for days. It was like solitary confinement, and like a prisoner who suffers through that cruel and unusual punishment it took her "so near the borderline of utter mental ruin that [she] could see over." She wrote the story to save other women from the same fate. She explains, "It was not intended to drive people crazy," as some doctors accused her of trying to do, "but to save people from being driven crazy, and it worked." It led doctors to reform their practices, to save their patients from the torture they had long subjected them to.

It's incredible, that she managed to do that. Writers try to change the world all the time, and it almost never works. Upton Sinclair wrote *The Jungle* in order to urge reform of labor practices, and all that came of it was the founding of the Food and Drug Administration. That was a pretty good thing, sure, but the workers got nothing, and they were the people the novel was meant to help.

Gilman hit the bullseye. And I don't think "The Yellow Wallpaper" would be as effective as it is in what it's trying to do if it weren't for its emphasis on the situation, rather than the character.

We never learn much about the narrator of "The Yellow Wallpaper." We know she's identified as a woman. We know she recently had a baby. But we don't know who she was prior to entering the room with the yellow wallpaper. She goes in, she gets lost in its awful patterns, and she has a series of hallucinations that are pregnant with significance on her way to trying to liberate herself by stripping the walls bare.

It is essential to the project of the story that it depend on its situation for momentum. It's important that as a character the narrator is something of a blank slate; it makes it much easier, then, for us to imagine any woman, any person, being placed in that situation and experiencing the same things.

If Gilman made this story about a character, if she spent much of the story's time on who she is, where she comes from, or whatever, it would obscure what she's up to, which is to reveal the cruelty of the situation she puts that character in. To give the character too much emphasis would throw the story off its axis and risk obscuring the point she wants to make.

·

HERMAN MELVILLE's "BARTLEBY, the Scrivener" is on the other side of the character-situation dichotomy.

Throughout "Bartleby," the workplace where the story is set gets a lot of attention, with its brick wall out the window, and the temperamental employees arrayed just so. The situation matters.

But it matters significantly less than the characters do, both the character of Bartleby and the character of the narrator.

Bartleby, as everyone knows, gets hired by the narrator to copy documents, to be a human photocopier, a drone. Soon after he is hired, he refuses to do any work whatsoever. "I prefer not to," he says instead, whenever his boss asks him to do something. When he's fired, he prefers not to vacate the premises, and he eventually just dies, which shakes the narrator to his core. His final cry of "Ah, Bartleby! Ah, humanity!" indicates, among other things, how the narrator has been altered irreversibly by his failure to do for Bartleby what needed to be done. And it's not at all clear what that was, the thing that needed to be done, which is in part what makes it a confounding and powerful story.

If you wanted to make a film adaptation of "Bartleby, the Scrivener," and take liberties with some aspects of it but keep the heart of the story beating at the same pace and with the same vitality, what would you do? You wouldn't take different characters and put them in the office where Bartleby was hired. Even if you included his absurd coworkers, you would not strike the same spark as the original.

You would strike that spark, though, if you took Bartleby and the narrator and put them in another situation.

It's what Jonathan Parker did when he directed an adaptation of the story in 2001. This *Bartleby* takes place in the modern era, with David Paymer playing the office boss and Crispin Glover playing Bartleby. Joe Piscopo is in it, too, but the point is, Bartleby in the movie is exactly who he is in the story. He and the narrator are all you really need.

The pair of them could be anywhere, and the tension between them would be the same generator with the same great power. You could make the narrator a zookeeper who hires Bartleby to clean shit out of gorilla stalls. You could make him a restaurant owner who hires Bartleby to wash dishes. The story could play out in much the same way, in any situation, as long as you kept the narrator and Bartleby.

Of course, if you change the setting, you get a different story. The situation *matters*; it's meaningful that Melville sets the story in an office on Wall Street. My point is, we can safely call this a story that concerns characters primarily, since it's where most of the stress falls.

•

I'VE NEVER WRITTEN anything with columns in it.

So here are two columns, featuring lists of stories that I put in one category or another. Some of the stories everyone knows, whereas others were written by my friends. They are great stories, and everyone should read them. If you've read them before, read them again.

Situation

Donald Barthelme, "The School"
George Saunders, "Sea Oak"
Katie Chase, "Man and Wife"
Kate McIntyre, "The Moat"
John Cheever, "The Enormous Radio"
Franz Kafka, "In the Penal Colony"
Aimee Bender, "The Rememberer"
Stephanie Carpenter, "The Sweeper"
Jack London, "To Build a Fire"
Karin Tidbeck, "Jagannath"
Gabriel Garcia Marquez, "The Handsomest Drowned Man in the World"
Stefanie Wortman, "Milk Rush"
Edgar Allan Poe, "The Masque of the Red Death"
Dionne Irving Bremyer, "Florida Lives"
Joe Aguilar, "Poles"

Character

Zora Neale Hurston, "The Gilded Six-Bits"
Tatyana Tolstoya, "On the Golden Porch"
Ted Chiang, "Story of Your Life"
William Gibson, "Burning Chrome"
Jayne Anne Phillips, "Black Tickets"
Chimamanda Ngozi Adichie, "The Thing Around Your Neck"
Evelyn Hampton, "Blondlot's Transformation"
Joanna Luloff, "Let Them Ask"
James Alan McPherson, "A Solo Song: For Doc"
Anton Chekhov, "The Lady with the Dog"
Nafissa Thompson-Spires, "Heads of the Colored People: Four Fancy Sketches, Two Chalk Outlines, and No Apology"
Erin Somers, "Ten Year Affair"

•

THERE ARE STORIES I don't know what column to place in—like "Wants," by Grace Paley.

A woman returns a library book that's long overdue, and on the steps of the library she meets her ex-husband. Together they rehash their marriage.

It's an incredible short story. If you haven't read it, you need to. But you've probably read it before, if you're reading this.

It's a story that confounds the distinction I'm arguing for throughout this essay. Is "Wants" guided more profoundly by the character who speaks to us throughout it, or is it led along by the situation she finds herself in, on those library steps, where her ex turns up?

I don't know!

If I had to put money on it, I'd say it's the situation. I think Grace Paley is a writer whose work in general thrives on situations. But in this case I can see making just as compelling an argument the other way.

In the end, of course, it doesn't really matter. Not at all.

It's important to have that in mind. I have it in mind.

All I'm doing here is projecting a blacklight onto short stories in order to see them in a slightly different fashion from the way we see them usually. This particular blacklight has its uses. But if you don't switch the blacklight off when you're done, if you read by it all the time, everything you look at will look wrong, and you'll hurt your eyes.

I'm as suspicious as anyone of the effort—even as I make that effort—to come up with new ways to create artificial categories for sorting complex and intricate works of art into different piles. It's reductive and it's unnecessary; and it's far more beneficial, enlightening, and fun to read a short story without letting this stuff cloud your perception of it.

But it has its uses. It has helped me out. It's worth devoting an essay to, I think. I mean, I hope it is.

•

THERE IS ONE more thing to add to this essay, one more thought I've had about this that I'm just as uncertain of as the rest of it, but which, once I had it, I couldn't shake.

Soon after it occurred to me that making this distinction between short stories was something worth doing, I wondered if it was possible to have a short story that is driven with equal force by its character(s) and its situation. And that is possible; maybe "Wants" is one of those stories.

But I wonder if the combination of equal parts character and situation sparks a chemical reaction that results in a novel.

It could be why, sometimes, when you start writing a story, you realize partway in that there's no way to contain in a short story all of the material that issues from the tension you're putting pressure on. A short story can't handle the combined, equal power of situation and character; it would be like putting the engine from a tractor-trailer in a Chevette.

Maybe the fundamental difference between the novel and the short story isn't length or scope or whatever. Maybe it's a difference you can see if you look under a text's hood to determine what's pushing it forward.

I really don't know.

One of the great things about not being a professor anymore is that I feel like it's okay to not know things and admit that. I can talk and write about stuff and not be afraid of seeming stupid. I can unabashedly use the word "stuff."

I don't *want* to seem stupid. I don't want to *be* stupid.

But I used to be afraid of being and seeming stupid constantly. I'm not really afraid of it at all anymore.

MARIA POULATHA

Take One

THE SEA WAS AS SMOOTH as a bar of soap last night. Three more refugee boats arrived, navigated by a constellation of lights that is our cluster of houses by the shore: a few vacation homes that have become permanent residences, a tavern that works on weekends and a converted boat shed that is a cozy loft for tourists, a trap for crabs in the winters.

I awake at dawn, as I do these days, and hear someone hollering fragments of Greek, English and Arabic. Somehow, the directions are understood as a boat is guided toward the tiny harbor where fishing boats named after saints or spouses are docked beside a family of geese with bewildering vocal chords. I pull on a dress and my husband's pilling sweater then walk over cats sleeping in the middle of the street. Yesterday's October morning I chased octopus out of its cave just to watch it shift from ash to gold to moss and then disappear in a hero's black cloak. Today it turned cold.

The boat is tied next to a rowboat named after our patron, St. Anna, and 50 people are stowed inside like socks in a drawer, trembling but smiling with elation and uncertainty. A handful of villagers are already there, salty fishermen plucked from storybooks, dough-plump women in house slippers and droopy cardigans and my first boyfriend who held my hand once at a dance when my mother wasn't looking, wearing a faded t-shirt that says 'Grab a Heiney' and orange rubber clogs. He pretends he doesn't remember me or perhaps he really doesn't remember much. He fell off his motor scooter years ago and his eyes loll in their sockets like languid buoys ever since.

The newcomers lift their children to us as they continue to crouch; no doubt some have soiled themselves on the grueling journey. They stagger out only after we've turned away to carry their damp children to folding tables covered with freshly washed clothes. We strip off soaked jumpers and nappies, wipe crusty noses and swaddle blanket after blanket.

Perhaps my husband is up, wondering if I have gone for a morning swim, a morning walk, anything to avoid the mornings. He is probably having hot toast on the balcony, looking at the silver line, like the trail of a slug, that the boat left on the surface of the perfect sea. Maybe he is swallowing butter and honey and frowning at the milky scar expanding like an aged stretch mark. He always kisses my belly in awe at the flat morning-sea-smoothness of it, thinking this is a compliment.

The baby in my arms tilts her head onto my shoulder, grows limp and purrs through a clogged nostril. I add friction to her back with my free hand then rock her to sleep as I sway and hum. The old boyfriend looks away, embarrassed. Everyone here is aware of my situation. A woman in velvet slippers and black knee-high socks whose husband and son shot each other in a hunting accident pats the baby's hair and I pull away instinctively. "Where is her mother?" she asks, a permanent look of dread on her face. I shake my head. The mothers, dry and changed, are sitting under a fig tree, breastfeeding or crushing crackers in their palms.

A fisherman whose face was formed by a child with wet sand and shards of seashells hollers, "Take her! Take her home!" The women look at me with solemn, complicit eyes. "We'll name her Anna!" he cries. I picture my husband, seeing me with a baby in my arms, as he has pictured me so many times and I smile and turn away from the old boyfriend, the stout women and the toothless fisherman.

I wonder if she can eat octopus yet, or the creamy eggs of urchins. I'll place baby octopuses on her skin so that she can feel multiple sucking kisses. The baby flips her head to the other side so that her breath is on my neck and it smells like biscuits and sea salt and something mysteriously mineral. If I were a dog maybe I would call it fear. The fear will fade as she forgets and we will drain any remains into the sea. The baby is warm now and I am boiling inside and throwing everything in: the ancient teas, the holy apples, the healing mantras, the injections, the silent mornings, the bloody waste month after month, the fabric of my husband's face sagging like the seams have been undone.

Baby in arms, I steadily make my way to a path that leads away from the harbor. Before I even step onto the thin trail, the child's mother spots me as she exits the makeshift changing room. Her eyes see mine and she knows. I see in her terror the recollection of every child-consuming hag from all her grim childhood fairytales. She marches over, past the women with pitchers of juice, past the tables full of clothes and past the staring men to remove her baby from my arms.

Aroused by her mother's scent, the infant begins to root. I try to smile at the woman but my body, warmed by the baby, grows cold and begins to shiver. Someone throws a blanket over my shoulders and it smells like cedar and cooking grease, which makes me feel sick so I throw it onto a mound of clothes and topple a pile of socks. I walk home, join my husband on the balcony and stare at the gaping blank of the horizon, waiting for it to bring up the next lifeboat.

TARA ISABEL ZAMBRANO

Cow's Tongue

—SOMEONE HAD LEFT A COW's tongue on our doorstep, the flesh dark pink, a row of flies on it like the line of hairs on Papa's chest. The stench was dense–my mother's mouth at the end of the morning lining curses all the way to the front door. Our maid brought a newspaper and swept the tongue on it with a broom. The flies rose in the air, annoyed.

Before the verandah was swiped clean with milky phenyl water, I got a brief glimpse of the tongue. In the back yard, I was kissing my neighbor, Akbar—my tongue deep in his mouth, sucking his Lucknow tehzeeb, the sparse beard on his cheeks tickling my chin until I heard the commotion, the sharp voice of my mother calling on to all the Hindu Gods.

"Hey Ram," she yelled, "who could do this to us?" I heard her panicked steps approaching the kitchen, her long sighs filled with rage and frustration.

"Stay, please." Akbar held my arm "I have cigarettes." In the background, my mother called my name. "Will be back soon." I pushed him out of the back door.

—later, Akbar described how his Ammi would have cooked the cow's tongue. Spices, yogurt to marinate, a slow roast. He swiped his tongue over his lips.

"Shh, we cremated the tongue, the broom and the newspaper. A local priest performed a cleaning ritual," I said softly. Akbar laughed at the last part, a little rueful, his tall bulk listed against the brick wall. The street ahead of us was empty at this hour, the heat appropriate for June. We exchanged the cigarette, the smoke curled in front of us like a fresh ghost. Then Akbar pulled me in, blew into my mouth. My lungs filled with a heady vapor.

"I wish you had a phone in your house," he said. "Then I'd call and whisper love songs into your ears." Akbar with this tattoo of a flame on his upper right arm, mostly covered under his white kurta. Akbar with a tang of mutton masala on his finger pads, Akbar with slim curved ribs that bent like a spring as he kissed my neck. After he let go, I collapsed, the smoke escaping of my mouth one wing at a time–a bird.

—during the month of Ramadan, I saw Akbar once during the day. I brushed his lips with mine. "Not when I'm fasting." He left me with those words. Shafts of neon-orange July light leaked through the branches of the mango tree in my back yard and melted into a soft dusk, just when it was time for him to open his fast. Arabic murmurs rose from his house. I had an urge to pull out a mat and sit in front of my favorite Lord Krishna and press my palms together in a prayer.

Another day it was only ten am and I was sweating a lot. Leaning against the brick wall where Akbar and I used to make out. A pre monsoon mist haunted the road ahead of my eyes. I turned my head every time the leaves brushed against the window as if someone were walking toward me. I waited for him and felt my mind drifting away to a place somewhere in the small of my back. My fingers traced his name on the uneven wall, scratched my palm.

—when Akbar's Ammi invited us for Eid, my mother refused to attend. "It was someone from their family who threw the cow's tongue on our doorstep."

Papa shook his head. "We'll go," he declared.

I shaved the hairs on my arms and legs, armpits, down from my navel. I used a curling iron–my hair like silk ribbons, bouncy on my cheeks and back. I knew Akbar's cousins would be there–especially Atif. Atif who winked at me on several occasions, Atif who was muscular with boring brown hair.

I plucked the hairs between my eyebrows and wore a tight golden blouse with a green, sparkling ghaghra, bare midriff.

Inside Akbar's home, I walked upstairs, waited at the door of his room. Downstairs, my Hindu parents mingled with their Muslim neighbors, being civil to each other's customs and traditions like past ten years since we moved in. Akbar was at the window, watching birds landing on the mango tree. When he turned around, he took me in his arms. I forgot about Atif. I kissed him and his lips were coral.

Above his backyard pool, the sky hung, cinnamon-smudged and Lucknow pure; flushed, frowning, galaxies in water. A shy-red sun dipped into the horizon.

—"you know we cannot be together, sweetheart," Akbar said. Annoyed, I swatted his lips as if a mosquito had landed on them even though I knew the truth–different religions, customs, traditions. My parents would die of shame, so would his. Blood rushed to my cheeks. I struggled to form words, so I looked away. He came close, nibbled my ears. Then he said my name, it boomeranged off my insides.

When I was ready to leave, Akbar gave me an audio cassette–a recording of his favorite Bollywood songs. "This is your Eidi," he said.

At home, I closed my eyes and listened to it. Songs from Hindi movies, ghazals, some reciting poetry from Faiz, Iqbal, Ghalib.

As if you are with me, just when
There is no one else around me.

The next time I saw Akbar was at his engagement to Rukhsana, his distant cousin. Her eyes hazel, her mouth wide, her thighs in the sharaara like trunks of the banana trees. Her anklets rang, the hem of her dress bumped over the floor as she walked–not too fast or slow and sat next to him. Akbar wore an embroidered sherwani, sleeves rolled up to his elbows like I liked. Akbar smiled and greeted his relatives, shook hands–the love-lacked look that scored his face. Akbar looked grown up, distant. Rukhsana pinched her waist to adjust her dress, quirked an eyebrow. Was she so much better than me–being Muslim and beautiful, someone who'd cook a cow's tongue whereas I'd cremate it even though I'd find it absurd?

When Rukhsana hugged me as Akbar's neighbor and friend, I don't know why but I wanted to shake her, slip her out of the party and teach her everything Akbar enjoyed. I wanted to touch that mole on her left cheek and wipe that bit of lipstick smeared on her side tooth. I was feeling so kind towards her I felt I could not be trusted.

—the mango tree looked like a dragon in darkness. "Sweetheart," Akbar said, pushed his tongue inside my mouth. Something rustled in the tree. I led his hand inside my blouse, between my legs, his skin warm as the soupy night. The lights in our homes turned off one by one, a mist illuminated their outlines. In distance cars honked, fat drops of occasional rain tapped on our heads. Later, we cleaned each other with old newspapers in a pile for kabadee wala, a scrap collector. Moonlight leaked out of us.

It was past midnight when I showered, my bones taut like the elastic of my PJs. Tucked in bed, I thought of Rukhsana slipping a ring into Akbar's finger. Their heads joined together by their elders, the blessings for a lifetime. Then I imagined Akbar naked in my backyard a few hours ago before I fell asleep.

—mid October when Akbar and Rukhsana got married, I danced and got drunk with his friends who hid their liquor glasses in the trunks of their cars, their heads bobbing like microwaved popcorn. The loud music hollowed the night, his home lights whirlpooled. After the ceremony, Akbar and Rukhsana joined us, and she kept falling behind to catch his moves. But she had all the time in world to synchronize with him. On the other hand, I stayed close to Akbar, our torsos sewn, our arms buttoned, our bodies shuddered along an ethereal curve. How musky his hair smelled at the sideburns, Old Spice aftershave lingering on his chin. We had finished ten beers. *Remember this touch, remember this move. Remember this street, this time. Remember this feeling.* High on pride and foreplay, we continued until our laughter was harsh and our throats stung. Until I realized, I needed to go because my head was spinning, my body dry heaving. I walked past the bride, her eyes flushed with anger and tears as I tried to smile at her. It was late, everything blue, violet, as if a carnivorous flower opened in the sky, it's dark outer shell revealing the softer insides–the frilled edges, a row of curling tentacles. I kneeled by the edge of the driveway flecked red with the flaming hearts of the gulmohar tree and puked the dinner and alcohol, the warmth rising from inside and leaving in a stream—until my insides were empty, dry and coarse like a cow's tongue.

EMILY BANKS

Julius Caesar (1953)

In an unpublished document, T. S. Eliot admits
he never truly appreciated Shakespeare's *Julius Caesar*
till he saw the 1953 movie with Marlon Brando
as Marc Antony—and boy, me too. I was in middle school
when I saw that movie and I still know
the *Friends, Romans, countrymen* speech by heart and it's not
Shakespeare's fault. And sure, I wanted Brando
to look down his Roman nose at me, a devious
half-smile cracking his flat line of lips,
thought about touching the bulging grid
of his torso that gleamed like bronze when he lost
the toga for a gladiator's short skirt—but what I wanted more
was to put words in his mouth. I didn't long
to be a woman lounging nude in his villa so much
as I longed to be Shakespeare,
to pen a soliloquy so powerful it would make sweat
drip down his chest and condense on his upper lip
as he spoke it. I craved his hours spent
memorizing, reciting, losing his place and restarting,
bowing down in frustrated deference to every syllable.
Shakespeare's grave must have quivered
when it hit the screen. At first after I saw it I thought
I'd be a political speechwriter, imagined lingering
in the back of a great hall unseen, seeing
a crowd cheer for the man holding
my paragraphs at the back of his throat,
running his tongue along my precisely placed
commas, eager for the signal to release.
Poor Eliot, though, he could never come
and go like Michelangelo, whose beaten hands
measured the paradigm of masculine vigor
into being. For all his talent, couldn't make a man
like he wasn't. Couldn't get inside

a man's mouth like Shakespeare could.
I mean, why else would anybody *choose*
to be Catholic? In London, a scholar
lectured my seminar about Eliot's vow of celibacy,
how he *sublimated* his sex drive into poetry.
But I'm guessing that man never wrote
a poem, or else he didn't see the 1953
Julius Caesar with Marlon Brando as Marc Antony.

JOHN POCH

The Future of Love

Our bodies
turn us on,
turn on us

like Turner's
skies from seas
turn over

until waves
go whitecap.
Disaster

loves the past
but few love
the future,

except for
the dying
who believe

the present
hurting will
un-harden,

find harbor
in the way
a birdcage

on a dock
in shadow
beside a

giant ship
is open
and waiting

not for birds
but for a
museum

and your eyes
which look through
me, see, say:

Let's make love
under an
old black grand

piano
otherwise
known as night.

LANCE LARSEN

The Backpacks

Her legs, his arms, everything about their coupling
was impossible, her hair, his left shoulder,
the smashed-down grave they made in that meadow,
the coat they lay on, their movement like fish
chasing each other in bright shallows. Even the sky
lipped and lapped. Or was that just the breeze
plotting with my embarrassment? Impossible,
a pair of high schoolers trading their naked vows
in a field inside city limits, and me, a twelve-year-old
hoping to hunt lizards. Or was she Eve
and I wasn't yet born? Was he the first man
and I was one of the stumps I was hiding behind?
How could this be a weekday on the edge of town?
How could their bright bodies not start a fire?
I said they were naked. I meant almost naked.
She kept her shirt on, he wore a pink bandana
to tie back his hippy hair. I kept looking
and looking away, their backpacks slumped
like duffel bags. Hers orange, his purple with purple
stripes, same as mine back home. This happened
in an earlier century when you plucked dumb
colors from the rainbow and that's what you
shouldered all year. Were their packs filled
with drugs? Cans of stolen beer? With a flock
of pigeons waiting to be flung at the sky? Nothing
would have surprised me. Hidden doors opened,
between them, inside me. Then they stopped.
I expected their packs to burst into flame or turn
into soft rabbits and hop into dusk. Should I run?
No, staying low was safer. I closed my eyes
for as long as I could stand. Then opened them:
clothes finding their way back onto bodies,
meadowlarks keeping up their quaint Q & A.

Then he stood and helped her up, and they hoisted
their packs. Wait, the purple one belonged to her?
I felt scared and hot and shy and chosen.
Straps dug into her shoulders. Heavy packs.
The two of them must have come straight
from school, schlepping biology and American lit,
pouches bulging with calculators and flunked
tests, erasers and leaky pens, I tried to picture
it all, love notes and Chapstick, perfume
and smelly gym clothes and leftover carrots
and half sticks of gum, smokes. And lint, yes
lint, same as in mine. Gravity pulling at everything.
And me wanting to shoulder my share of it,
the heavy sky and cooling earth of it, the purple
that stayed purple even when you closed your eyes.

GARY FINCKE

After the Great War

A child creates a daily maze,
each, he says, a new version
of purgatory. Finished, he asks
his mother to escape
without lifting her pencil.

They live alone, the studio
small enough to memorize,
the corridors on each floor
straight and right-angled
as a toddler's puzzle.

When she struggles, retracing,
he imagines her prayer.
When she exits, he believes
she has managed penance.
Always, he times her.

School is noise and nuns,
as simple as a sidewalk
broken by numbered streets.
Mass is an unsolvable
labyrinth of soloed Latin.

One evening, his mother,
the pencil still pressed
to the paper, declares
there is no solution.
Mute, he taps his watch.

The apartment is cluttered
with hesitation and sighs.
When she retraces again,
the line thickens until it fills
each alley, until it's hell.

MICHAEL DUMANIS

The Kidnapped Children

Some of us remember our parents
as shadows capable of song
who smelled of salt each time they leaned toward us
their foggy branches. We were well along
on the ill-defined journey, following their kind
yet strident cadences. We had become accustomed
to the mouthful of names they prepared in the dark,
luminous flower, creased feather, my hoped-for one.
Who was it then that dragged us over stones?
Now the rats are in charge, a pageant of gnaw.
They flounce across the avenue, rally the square,
stand upright on hind legs to gauge the crowd.
The rats are winning. Their shadows swoon
over the parking lot of the abandoned mall.

First, we were taken by surprise, away, for granted,
but later, taken care of, taken in.
A bath was run. We were prohibited from drowning.
A nurse made rounds to clip our fingernails.
Some of us remember only now and then
the prickly scarf our neck slipped through
one nightfall of wind, and the soft eyes
like stars we fail to place, stars we can't locate
in a face that must have held them. Some of us
have no idea who we are, whose neck
we cradled as we piggybacked, and we know better
than to ask help of the wind that propels us, the sunlight
dissolving the snow. Who anyone is
no one knows anymore. At least we have one another.

A Lake in Vermont

A lake is a depression.
I bob up and down,
a person who splutters,
a person who coughs

out of my windpipe into the sharp light,
lily pads choking
the velveteen water.
Each consecutive day

I know less what I'm after.
Each consecutive lake
I float longer and farther
as the lungs swell to their capacity

with unsustainable love
for each subarctic bluet damselfly,
every stray sweetflag
spreadwing dragonfly. I may

or may not reach enlightenment.
I have no memoirs, no memory.
The retina reacts to images.
The mountains ring me.

LIS SANCHEZ

In Caguas; the New Dead

Carla Medina de Sánchez, September 6, 1899*

Repulsed by idleness
and elbowed out by the old dead,
the new dead come riding after us
on their stiff green feathers.

Famished, tattered,
they fasten like thumbs to the blasted
hands of the flamboyán. This one *be-weeting,*
with her garden snail knees,
with her garish berry throat, with her pointless noise
and laundress claws

brings to mind my scandalous cousin Pilar.
At the first sizzle of cassavas she'd sweep in,
shimmering inside the green shawl
she washed for the jealous wife of the hacendado
before the wife tossed the shawl in the ditch atop Pilar, who
for a fortnight rolled her eyes at the caterpillars
gnawing her eyelids, so that later, she hardly
recognized herself.

But look now: this little bird
arcs over the watery street, stuffs her bill
with moths, she swallows centipedes whole,
snaps a lizard in half, a tarantula, a rat. She chomps,
scans the ground—inside a puddle—something
green, taunting. She pounces, stabs.
It stabs back.

---

* Twenty-eight days after San Ciriaco, the most destructive hurricane in Puerto Rico's history, made landfall.

She plucks out its eye; blood
geysers from her eye socket.
There's a downpouring of birds.
With a roil of feathers,
with hissing and jabbing,
everyone flaps and stabs.

That's how you spot the new dead:
they can't get enough of themselves.

NIKI HERD

"Objects of Care," Stony Island Arts Bank, Chicago, 2018

The abandoned bank building now museum on the South
Side of Chicago. On display—ICONIC: ARTISTS INTERPRET
50 YEARS OF THE BLACK PANTHER PARTY. In the main
room the words DANGER RIOT, a Shepard Fairey
double-painting EMBRACE JUSTICE, next, a floor-to-ceiling
X in yellow neon on the main wall, everything on display
translated into a raised fist. It's easy to walk past
the small room off the main exhibit, yellow caution tape
guarding entry, inside a mound of wooden planks,
teddy bears, dirty, an old vault visible & open.
Nothing remarkable to the eye until
the docent says: CLEVELAND GAZEBO TAMIR
& this is when sight begins to grieve its own condition;
how swiftly it barrels toward worth, unworth, guilt.
This is the closest she will get to writing a love poem
about the city in which she was born & damn why
does it have to be an elegy? The weight of wooden
planks & bright stuffed animals carried across two state lines,
from the Cudell Recreation Center to Stony Island Arts Bank.
When she returns to the yellow tape, the tombstone—
museum labels are called tombstones—notes the word SACRED,
asks visitors to be mindful of photographs & such & when asked
about the wood, what kind, the docent says most likely cedar—

KELLY MOFFETT

Into and Away

June screeches in as a hawk.
The dog lifts its overly confident leg.

The morning bends in prayer
or it is begging.

A shape fills the window.

It could be mother
or mother's fear.

The hoof of a deer imprints
the day like memory.

What listens is another matter.

Magritte Says Mystery Means Nothing

You disrobe in the backseat of my memory.
I cover up what I can when I can.

Through the window the evening
trips into its hole and hides there.

This is all wrong,
says the answer rising from tomorrow.

Everyone, even you, wants to be believed.
Belief a bird feather mother said not to touch.

What takes off is already in the horizon.
Take it back. Take all of it back.

Blackbeard

"The treatment will be painful," the specialist told Juliet's parents, "but it will be worth it in the end. You'll have your daughter back."

"Our daughter back," said Juliet's father.

Juliet's mother turned to her father and said, "Could you imagine having our Juliet back?" Her eyes were damp behind her tortoise-shell glasses.

"I'm right here," said Juliet. She was sitting between her parents on the hard leather couch, across the desk from the specialist.

The specialist said, "You're not yourself, Juliet. You haven't been yourself for months. It's my job to bring your old self back."

The specialist had a pale, squishy face. Juliet wanted to press her thumbs into that face, to see if there was bone beneath all that skin, or if he was the same all the way through, like Play-Doh. Then, as she watched, Blackbeard's face came to hover holographically over the specialist's. Juliet couldn't look at a man for longer than a few moments without the face of Blackbeard sliding down over his like a mask. The first few times this happened, she'd felt herself retreating inward, pitching into her own body as though into a well, but she'd found that anything could come to feel ordinary if it happened often enough.

"Once we know the device has worked," said the specialist to Juliet, "once we know you won't hurt yourself again, you can go back to school. Would you like that?"

"I'd like that," said Juliet, because that was what he wanted her to say, and she wanted him to stop talking. Really, she couldn't have cared less about the seventh grade. She only wanted to lie on her bed with her door closed, where Blackbeard couldn't find her, where she could be free of him, if only for a little while.

They were in a little office in a tall building in the city. Behind the specialist, Juliet could see the park and the trees growing in it, leafless and black, as though they had been inked onto the sky. They snagged at the linty clouds. There was a Blackbeard sitting cross-legged on a bench by the fountain, his face hidden behind a newspaper. She could see his woolly eyebrows beneath his orange hat. Juliet knew he was waiting for her to come out of the building so that he could follow her home. Then he stood, scattering pigeons like iron filings. He closed his newspaper and he wasn't Blackbeard at all. Of course he wasn't. It had been months since Juliet last saw Blackbeard, the real Blackbeard, and he wasn't coming back, she told herself, as she always told herself, though she couldn't make herself believe it.

As the elevator bore her back down into the city, Juliet looked into the closed doors, which were scored with scratches and grooves, and saw herself with her parents standing behind her. Beside them was the box containing the machine. As Juliet looked, a horde of Blackbeards swam up out of the murky brass. She took in their wild eyebrows, their red mouths like sugared cranberries behind thickets of facial hair.

"What's wrong?" said her mother's voice. She sounded muffled, as though she were speaking through a wall.

"Nothing," said Juliet. She closed her eyes against all those Blackbeards, and when she opened them the doors had parted and she was standing in the lobby. Outside was the street. A cab pulled up to the curb and a Blackbeard stepped out, wrapping a scarf around his neck.

Juliet knew that as she and her parents walked to the car there would be Blackbeards on every corner, Blackbeards framed in the windows of each passing bus. The world was brimming with Blackbeards and she was so tired. If she had her way, she would remain in this vestibule forever, with the elevator behind her and the street beyond the glass doors. But she couldn't remain in the vestibule. The world wouldn't let her. She knew it was either in or out, and whichever she chose, the Blackbeards would find her all the same.

•

Her parents strapped the box containing the machine to the roof of the car, like a Christmas tree. Then they returned to the farmhouse, where Juliet's father spent the evening assembling the machine. Juliet watched TV on her father's laptop until all of the characters became Blackbeard, an ensemble of sneering Blackbeards, and then she turned it off and stared at the blank screen, at her own reflection smeared across it like paint, and wanted to hurt herself again.

Her father untangled the wires, screwed the parts together, drilled eye hooks into the ceiling. Then there it was: a lightbulb big as a dinner plate, hanging over Juliet's bed from a thick braid of wires. The bulb was set into a hood of black metal, which made it look mysterious. All the wires fed into a large black box with several dials on it.

"Great work, honey," said Juliet's mother.

"It's ugly," said Juliet. She'd always had such a lovely room, with the coverlet of eyelet lace, the silver pitcher on the vanity, and now it was ruined.

"You must be tired, Juliet," said her mother, reaching out to pet Juliet's hair.

"It's not even eight," said Juliet, flinching from her mother's hand, but it was clearly time for bed, from the way her parents were looking at her, sick with hope and anticipation.

So she put on her pajamas and brushed her teeth. Her mother combed her hair and braided it. Then Juliet got beneath her covers and her parents switched on the lamp. The bulb shone deep red. It radiated a vengeful heat that warped the air like old glass. Everything was now red. Juliet's parents were dyed crimson, the shadows sharp beneath their eyes and noses. When they smiled, their teeth were rose-colored.

Juliet cringed from the light. "Does it have to be that hot?"

"You know it does," said her mother. "Don't you want to be yourself again?"

"Of course I do," said Juliet. She was so tired of questions with only one answer.

Juliet's father said, "Sleep well, then, Juliet. We're going to burn it out of you, all that bad stuff, and you'll be your old self again."

"We're so excited to have your old self back. Everything will be just like it was before."

Juliet could see they really believed this. They really thought it would go back to the way it was before. But Juliet knew the treatment wouldn't work, that it would fail like all the others. Only she knew her old self was in the cottage at the bottom of the yard, where Blackbeard had left her. But her parents knew nothing about Blackbeard. Juliet had tried to tell them many times but the words always got gummed up in her throat.

Juliet's parents kissed her forehead, and then they shut the door and locked it from the outside. This was what Juliet's parents had to do, to keep her safe. To keep her from hurting herself again. She wouldn't be let out until morning. She didn't mind that the door was locked. At least Blackbeard couldn't get in.

Branches scraped the house like fingernails. The heat from the lamp lashed her face like she'd opened an oven door. She felt as though her tongue might crumble in her mouth. She discarded her blankets, then shucked off her pajamas, until she lay on the bare mattress in her underwear.

The world outside was quiet and pristine, slaked with light from the pale, high moon. The apple trees, sheathed in ice, gleamed like porcelain. The creek's black banner sliced through the perfect white. Juliet longed for that cool, that calm. Inside her room, everything was hot and red, like the inside of a mouth.

She had to make it stop, the lamp. She tried to pull it down from the ceiling, but there were too many wires, braided too thick, and the bulb was so bright. Her eyes were dazed with bursts of orange the size of tangerines.

"Mom," she wept. "Dad." She pounded the locked door with her fists. "Please, let me out," she said.

When she turned around, Blackbeard was in the rocking chair in the corner.

His hands were folded over his belly. He rocked slowly back and forth. Juliet saw the flash of his teeth behind his beard and she was gone again, plunging into that ocean inside herself.

It was just as she remembered. He stood from the chair and slunk toward her. He reached for his belt, his fingers fat and red as plums. She was up against the door, and she was in the cottage again, with the rusty box spring leaned up against the wall, the lightbulb rattling like a fly caught in a jar.

When he came close enough, so close she could smell meat on his breath, she pushed him, and found that he didn't resist her, but stepped back, his expression unchanged. She pushed him again and again—his eyes wide and blue, almost lovely; his hands lifting as though to cup her face—until he went toppling out the window, fell with a tinkling of glass, and everything was finally quiet, except for the hissing of the lamp.

•

THE REST OF the night spent itself over many hours. Juliet lay on her side, facing the window. Icicles lengthened from the eaves. Patterns of frost grew across the remaining pane of glass, delicate as lace. As the sun rose, the ice went copper-colored. Snow gusted through the hole in the window and formed a glittering sheet across the floor.

Then, somehow, it was day. The lamp had gone out. The bulb was pale and benign in its black hood. Juliet sat up in her bed. She was wearing nothing but her underwear atop the mattress, with the winter air spilling in through the broken window. She wrapped herself in her quilt, slid to her feet, and stood shivering in the thin, strange light. The sun was little and hard, like a pearl. She looked down at the ground and saw something black in the snow. It was the toe of a boot, one of the shiny boots Blackbeard wore. She would have known those boots anywhere. She'd looked at them for long enough in the cottage. She stared hard at the bulb of leather, her heart hammering against her collarbone. It couldn't be, but perhaps it was. Perhaps Blackbeard was really dead. Perhaps the man who had visited her room last night hadn't been a figment of the night's fever but had instead been the real Blackbeard, come to claim her at last. After all, she'd felt the substance of him against her hands, had watched his red face grow small as he plunged into the bone-bleached dark.

Juliet heard the scritch of the key being inserted into the padlock on her door, and the handle turned, and there were Juliet's parents, still in their pajamas. They took in the shattered window, Juliet barefoot on a scrim of snow, blue with cold.

"Juliet," said her father, surveying her cautiously, "are you better?"

The sight of her parents standing there–their dear pajamas; their dear, worried faces–made tears prick in her eyes.

"Well?" demanded her mother.

"I'm better," said Juliet, because what else could she say.

•

IN THE NIGHTS that followed, Blackbeard didn't return again. The hours were long and sweltering, but she was mercifully alone.

After three nights beneath the lamp, Juliet began to develop blisters, great weeping sores that opened like eyes on her hands and feet and on the soft skin of her stomach. Each morning her mother dabbed ointment on the sores and taped new bandages over them. She said, "This is all worth it." She kissed each bandage to make the hurt better, and Juliet pretended that was enough.

Each morning Juliet looked out the window and checked that the boot was still there, poking out of the snow, and it was. She never dared go closer. She didn't think she could bear to look at his face. It was the boot that allowed her the first calm she'd felt in months. Throughout the day, she returned many times to the window, and each time she saw the boot was still there, she felt relief zing through her body like she'd touched cold metal with her tongue.

•

ON THE FOURTH day of her treatment, she ate two slices of toast without vomiting afterward, and her mother wept with joy. On the fifth, she walked to the mailbox at the bottom of the driveway and did not once did she see Blackbeard shifting in the woods.

On the eighth night, Juliet lay awake beneath the lamp. The heat hardly bothered her anymore. What she still couldn't tolerate was the thirst. She drained the pitcher on the vanity and still felt totally unsatisfied. She went to the door, turned the handle, and to her shock, it opened. Her parents had forgotten to lock her in. She took a step into the hall. She knew she shouldn't, but it was so beguiling, that clear, crisp dark.

And then she was standing barefoot in the snow. She didn't feel cold. The heat of the lamp clung like static to her skin. Snow spun all around her. It snagged in her eyelashes and melted down her face. She could hear each snowflake colliding with the earth, could hear individual pine needles clanking like chains. It was too much. She packed a handful of snow into her mouth. Her teeth jolted with pain; her mind went blissfully blank.

She looked back and there was the farmhouse, her parents enclosed within. Blackbeard was there, too, in the garden, beneath the snow. And now, before her, was the cottage at the bottom of the yard. She was standing on the threshold. The door was ajar. Her pulse battering in her ears, her blood hot and quick, she nudged it open and let herself in.

It was smaller than she remembered. She felt as though she hadn't been here in many years, though really it hadn't been six months. There was the little cot with its hard, filthy mattress. There was the bushel of pool noodles, there was the glass table with a dusty cloth draped over it, patterned with roses. It was like a room preserved in an antique photograph: anachronistic, somehow, a place that should no longer exist. But of course it existed, thought Juliet. It existed still and it always would.

She'd thought there might be some sign of Blackbeard in the cottage–a scent of him on the air, a footprint stamped into the dust, a cigarette wedged between the floorboards–but there was nothing. She found herself doubting that Blackbeard had ever existed. But there, in the corner, was the blanket. She remembered the blanket, with its coppery smell, the wool fibers rougher than they ought to have been. It had provided no warmth, that blanket. If anything, it had trapped the cold she'd felt in her chest as Blackbeard had draped it over her, when he was done with her. The act had belied a tenderness that was worse, somehow, than his hands on her shoulders, than his pale eyes tunneling into hers.

There was a shape beneath the blanket. A faint slope, a slight figure in repose. She hardly dared believe it. Against the voice telling her she should not, should leave, should let the blanket keep its secret, she leaned down and picked it up.

She didn't know what she'd expected. A younger, better Juliet, curled warmly beneath the blanket, lamb-like in sleep? A stoic, desiccated corpse? But there was nothing beneath the blanket, just air. The old Juliet wasn't waiting somewhere for Juliet to find her and bring her back. Blackbeard had broken her irreparably, had vanished who she was before.

For a moment, Juliet merely stood, the blanket in her hands. Snow piled up against the cottage, embedding it like a tooth in a gum. It lay over the orchard like gauze. Perhaps the snow would just keep falling, would wipe it all away: the cottage, the orchard, the farmhouse, the world. Erase it, reverse it. That would be all right. If it was wiped away, Juliet could start over. She could do it all exactly right. That first day, when she saw Blackbeard's truck idling across from the bus stop, she would run, she would tell her mother and father, she wouldn't hold it all inside, wouldn't tell herself it was okay, and perhaps then she would never end up in the cottage at the bottom of the yard with Blackbeard's shadow slanting over her, his sticky red lips smiling around his crooked teeth. His smell of meat. She would be better, she wouldn't want to hurt herself anymore, and her parents would be happy, and life would be the way it was supposed to be, the way she'd thought it would always be, when she was little, when she was her old self again.

But the snow eventually did stop falling. The world went still and the sun began to rise, pink like the inside of a shell. Juliet stepped out of the cottage. She left the door slightly open, in case she'd been wrong, somehow, in case her old self really did come back, had just been hiding. So that her old self could angle through the open door and come back to her, could fit herself back into Juliet's body as though into a well-worn coat. Juliet knew this wouldn't happen, but she needed a little hope to warm her as she made the long walk home.

•

AFTER A MONTH, Juliet completed her last treatment. Her father took down the lamp, packed it back into its box, and stored it in the attic. Juliet's blisters scabbed and began to heal, though Juliet knew they would leave scars behind, faint silver scars like blushes of moonlight on her skin.

"Let's never speak of this again," said Juliet's mother, gathering Juliet into her arms and kissing the top of her head.

"Yes," said Juliet, "I'd like that."

She no longer saw Blackbeard in the face of every passing man, no longer wanted to hurt herself so badly it was like she couldn't breathe until she did it. She was all right, as long as Blackbeard's boot was still in the garden, reminding her that she'd done it, that she'd made him let her be.

She grew so used to the sight of the boot outside her bedroom window that the reassurance of it barely registered anymore. Her glances became cursory, like checking her hair in the mirror before she left the house. And then one morning, months after her last treatment, the boot was gone.

It must be there, she thought, looking down at the expanse of merciless white. It must simply be buried deeper beneath the snow. But Juliet knew that it was April, that the snow was finally melting, and so Blackbeard was gone, or maybe he'd never been there, maybe that hadn't been his boot at all, but a stone or a slick of ice, a manufactured comfort she'd been living with for months as Blackbeard had been out there, waiting.

Juliet made up her mind. This time, she'd tell her mother and father. But she came downstairs to find the house done up with banners and balloons. There were sheets of tinsel twinkling from the ceiling and streamers twined around the bannisters. Juliet's mother was wearing a cardboard hat affixed to her chin with an elastic band. She said, "Juliet, we're so happy you're better, your father and I. You're so much better that we're throwing you a birthday party."

The light off the tinsel was far too bright; Juliet shielded her eyes with her hand. She said, "But my birthday was in September."

Her mother said, "You were sick then, and you're not sick anymore, and so now we're going to celebrate. All of your aunts and uncles will be here, and the girls from your class, and their mothers, too."

"Okay," said Juliet.

"They'll be here any minute," said Juliet's mother, turning to scan the yard outside. The sky was a cement wall. There were balloons tied to the mailbox, marking their driveway for the imminent guests. The balloons jostled and yanked in the wind. Juliet searched the road for a green truck, searched the orchard for movement between the apple trees.

The guests arrived. Juliet stood very still as the swarm of them seethed around her. She was assaulted by perfume, by whiskered kisses from balding uncles. She heard ice cubes clinking in glasses, tongues moving wetly in mouths. Outside, the snow was melting, grass tunneling up through the dirt. Water ribboned through the orchard toward the cottage at the bottom of the yard. Blackbeard could be anywhere. He could be dragging himself out of the garden, dusting snow from his denim jacket.

It was time for the birthday cake. Juliet sat at the end of the dining room table, and they all stood around it, her neighbors and friends, her uncles and aunts, and sang her a birthday song, their voices jangling and loud. Juliet wanted to cover her ears and wait for the song to be over.

Her mother and father came out of the kitchen, carrying the platter with the birthday cake on it. It was a three-layer cake piped with buttercream swirls. The icing said, WE'VE MISSED YOU, JULIET! There were thirteen candles on the cake. Juliet felt at once far too old and far too young to be thirteen.

It was then, over her parents' shoulders, that she saw him coming up the drive. Blackbeard in his denim jacket, Blackbeard with his yellow teeth. Blackbeard's mouth like a cherry candy, like a bloodstain on a white cloth.

She'd called him Blackbeard after the pirate from the story. She didn't know the story well, had heard the name only once—in the bunkhouse of a summer camp, a flashlight held beneath a chin—but it was what she'd thought of when he'd reached for his belt. He'd hung above her in the sepia-toned dim of the cottage and she'd said, Blackbeard, and he'd just blinked. It was this that had thrown him, she would think later. Not the tears, not the promises she'd made to any gods that might be passing over—that she would be kinder to her parents, that she would try her best in math when she started seventh grade in September. What had gotten him was that she'd given him his name. It was only then that he'd rolled off of her, that he'd done up his belt and settled the blanket over her shoulders and grunted at her, Go. And she'd gone, shedding the blanket onto the floor, leaving Blackbeard on the cot with his head in his hands, and she hadn't come back, not for many months, until she'd returned in search of a girl who had stopped existing a long time ago.

As Blackbeard neared, she saw that there were many more men behind him, more Blackbeards. They were different men but really they were all the same. She had the same feeling, looking at them, that she'd had when she'd first seen Blackbeard, all those months ago: a sense that he'd come to collect on a debt, on a promise Juliet didn't remember making.

The Blackbeards were well past the cottage now. Juliet knew there would be no stopping them. She supposed she'd always known they were coming. She supposed she'd known that the rest of her life would be marked by Blackbeards, Blackbeards who would hurt her in ways both large and small but hurt her nonetheless, who would seek her out because of things she could not control nor fully understand. They were coming for her across the snow. Any moment they would find her.

But for now there was the birthday cake, the haze of candle smoke, the rosy faces of the party guests.

"Make a wish, Juliet," said her mother.

So Juliet thought up a wish. She held it in her mouth like a dog holds a live bird: softly, invisibly, cradled on her tongue. She took in the last of the light from the birthday candles; the love in the eyes of her parents; the last notes of the birthday song, which still shimmered damply on the air, like kettle steam. She filled her lungs with breath and extinguished the flames.

Translation Folio

JESÚS AMALIO LUGO

Translator's Introduction

David M. Brunson

VENEZUELA IS FACING ONE OF the world's worst humanitarian and economic crises. Over six million people—more than 18 percent of the population—have fled Venezuela since Hugo Chávez rose to power in 1999, beginning a process of democratic backsliding that has resulted in Venezuela's current situation. In recent years, especially since the death of Chávez and his replacement by Nicolás Maduro, the Venezuelan economy has collapsed, the rate of migration has accelerated, and human rights have deteriorated further. As of 2019, the inflation rate of the Bolivar has reached 10 million percent, and despite recent attempts by the government to stabilize the economy through new price controls and the removal of six zeros from its currency system, the economy remains in freefall. This hyperinflation has led to severe food shortages and hunger: a single carton of eggs now costs more than a month's earnings on the country's minimum wage. 96% percent of the population lives in poverty. Only 3% of the population is food secure. According to a 2020 Human Rights Watch estimate, 18,000 people have been killed by Venezuelan security forces since 2016. Intimidation, torture, arbitrary detention, and extortion are commonplace. Corruption is the norm. The regime maintains power through black market endeavours like drug trafficking, money laundering through the front of social programs such as food assistance programs, and the illegal extraction of gold from the Venezuelan Amazon through strip mining and the murder of Indigenous groups in their territory.

Those who remain in the county are often reliant on an external source of income from family members living abroad. Many of those without the resources to send family members overseas live in extreme poverty. Because of the financial necessity of migration, there has been an enormous and ever-increasing influx of Venezuelans to other countries. The first people to leave their homeland often belonged to Venezuela's younger, educated generation. This was the generation that came of age during Chavismo, witnessing the slow collapse of their country. This wave began in 2015 as migrants sought new opportunities in professional careers, sent money home to their families, and built lives in more stable countries. Since then, Venezuela's migration crisis has accelerated, and immigrants have often been met with hostility. Xenophobic rhetoric by authoritarian leaders such as Donald Trump and Sebastián Piñera, as well as candidates such as Chile's José Antonio Kast, has led to new laws that deny temporary protections and visas to migrants, while simultaneously using Venezuela's suffering as an example to discredit popular progressive movements within their own countries. Meanwhile, authoritarian left-wing governments in the region such as Cuba, Nicaragua, and Peru, deny the human rights violations and election fraud under Maduro's regime, and view Venezuelan migrants as spies, threats, or traitors. Peru's president, Pedro Castillo, has even planned mass deportations of Venezuelan migrants to "return them to the fatherland." Trapped between these different incarnations of xenophobia and extremism, many Venezuelans are left without a country. Whereas the first migrants arrived to jobs, visas, and new lives, today's migrants sleep in metros, parks, and airports, and are often the victims of violence. This September in Iquique, a city in northern Chile, the police forcefully removed an immigrant encampment of 100 undocument families from a public park. The next day, Chilean nationalists attacked the families and burned their belongings while singing the national anthem.

Given this reality, what is the role of the poet? While translating these poems, I began to think of the differences between the reportage of journalism and the reportage of poetry. While the importance of good journalism is undeniable, it at times fails to encapsulate the hearts and minds of its subjects—especially when an unfathomably large number of humans are involved. The reportage of journalism instead relies on metanarrative as its primary mode of discourse, but this comes with its own set of shortcomings. The phrase "six million Venezuelan migrants are now living abroad" fails to encapsulate the personal, intellectual, and emotional histories that hide behind the thin veneer of statistics. It fails to account for the emotional weight of watching a country slowly fail, of watching friends and family disappear one by one, of leaving a country behind forever. The phrase "extrajudicial killings" can't account for each story of each life lost or the emotional toll on the lives left behind, of daily commutes that pass by jails and interrogation sites, of the ever-present hunger. Poetry is a different kind of reportage, one that struggles to find balance between bearing witness to atrocity and of rising above this trauma as a fully-realized human, one who has lived these experiences but who will not be defined by victimhood. It struggles with being a participant in a mass exodus and with retaining one's own individuality, of being more than just a number. The extreme politicization of the discourse surrounding Venezuela, and more importantly, of the lived experiences of the Venezuelan people, seeks to erase their humanity in favor of ideology. Poetry does the opposite—it elevates their voices and shows their humanity, both shared and individual.

Many Venezuelan poets are now living abroad, unable to return to the violence of their home. Rising above this is not an easy task. For that, it must be the task of poetry. To escape is to be in exile, and exile takes many forms. Exile is both physical and mental. Jesús Amalio Lugo writes that "I live in a diluvial southern city / where my psychologist diagnoses me with a vegetable-like sickness / He tells me / 'You have Seasonal Affective Disorder / You need more sun.'" For Lugo, the only consolation is to think of the sunny Caribbean, where "all / those corpses / don't get enough sun either." Despite the darkness of their social context, these poems also exhibit an extraordinary hope, found through nature, through art, through family, through quietness and self-reflection. In the face of the migration, the statelessness, and the violence of a failed revolution, perhaps the role of poetry is to teach us to walk "slowly as if sleeping / and [to] accept that to be / earth's most eternal creature / you must build yourself for defense / never to attack."

JESÚS AMALIO LUGO : Three Poems

[I have a collection of powerful objects]

I have a collection of powerful objects
from different celestial sources
a rosary of fluorescent plastic
a letter from my dead father
various birthday cards
a pearl that is the moon—only my friends and I know—
a paraplegic turtle named Vértigo who sleeps beside my cousin
a compass that, in spite of magnetism, points south
and a notebook where I try—truthfully—to write without literary intentions
All of my objects are legacies of God
What is God?
I get a bit tangled up when explaining my faith
What if I'm an atheist? I don't believe, because I believe
My beliefs are so many that I might have messianic tendencies
I believe:
I believe in the effectiveness of my sister Miriam praying the rosary in the middle
    of 3:00 PM traffic
I believe in the certainty of my other sister—Milagro—who believes she speaks
    with God when she closes her eyes
I believe in my mother taming enemies with her holy card of the Lion Saint
I believe in Nadia's Buddhism
God works better if we breathe from the belly
I believe in Bach's flowers
calluna vulgaris and mimulus guttatus
in more chocolate, four times a day, before sleep
I believe in the aging women who dance like teenagers every Thursday at 7
I believe in Mrs. Aida and her Sunday prayers in Maravén
I believe in the tasks that my father entrusts me when I dream
I believe that, when I was 11, I saw a fairy trapped in the power lines in front of
    my house
And yes, I confess before you brothers of science and power
that I believe in a pair of Bible verses
and two or three poetry collections

No, I am not religious
but when they sing my country's anthem, it's like prayer
When I speak of my people, and their Marquezian situations
I preach
When I speak of my friends and family
—with their devine eccentricities—
I am not an immigrant, I am a missionary
Because God is all of the people that love me
God is all of those I love
And if my name is Jesús, it's because my father is God
as are my mother and my sisters
Jehová, Yavé, Patricia, Mariana
Angélica, Aneidis, and Ana
So numerous are their names
Uncountable their miracles
No, I am not religious, but each of their words is a new verse in my testament
A moment with them: another aggregate to my sacred memory
That's why I ask you lord
that if, for having a sinful and reckless mind,
I fall back into hell
protect the many hands that would burn

to lift me out

Slowly

Tortoises know they can't control their destiny
they accept that someday we'll come and flip them over
or paint ironic eagles across their shells
For those who can breathe
for over one-hundred-sixty years
men will always be children
and their problems childish
Tortoises
hard in their mute calm
long-lived and slow
bearers of the secrets of longevity
teachers of impenetrability
though soft and sentimental
chose through evolution to observe silence
They're my favorite animal
I wish I learned
from lipless mouths
the secret of walking slowly as if sleeping
and of accepting that to be
earth's most eternal creature
you must to build yourself for defense
never for the attack

My name is nobody
and everybody calls me Nobody.
—The Odyssey

If for once feeling were a choice
I would have chosen to suffer
a more romantic kind of pain
I would have shouted—Ulysses Syndrome!
      and strangers would tie me to anxiolytic masts
and stop my return home
from these unhealthy borders
In this way my pain would be rooted in the Ancient Greek
and my bradycardia would be
an absolute alibi
for my pretentious disengagement
However
I live in a rainy southern city
where my psychologist diagnoses me with a vegetable-like sickness
He tells me
"You have Seasonal Affective Disorder
You need more sun"
"I'm neither hero
              nor man?"—I ask
"Only a vegetable," he responds
and prescribes me a visit to a greenhouse
I grumple
Where will I go?
I never loved the rain
I never should have left
never
How can I escape through these
partly-cloudy windows?
What train is going to plow across the south?
I should console myself by thinking of the Caribbean
with its hunger
and its guns
and its dead

Surely all
         those corpses
don't get enough sun either

Translated from the Spanish by David M. Brunson

MARK HALLIDAY

Cubs Fans

That year when we went to six or seven Cubs games
it wasn't that we cared about the Cubs, or about baseball.
Baseball is ridiculous, and "the Cubs" is a concept
absurdly dependent on the uniforms, the caps,

but we wanted to feel positive in a simple emphatic way
about some vivid patch of experience
and we wanted to share this positivity

and going to Cubs games seemed the available form of
ostensibly entertaining activity easy to refer to,
we could say "We saw the Cubs game last night"
and people always nodded and smiled
as if our choice made obvious good sense
and we said often that we loved Wrigley Field
because we knew this to be a venerable aesthetic view

(though my sharpest memory is of enjoying the Polish sausages)

but we didn't really care when the Cubs won or lost,
and that one time when they made a triple play
involving a line drive to the second baseman
I was looking at my Polish sausage
and when I stood up and roared because
everyone else stood up and roared
I got mustard on my thighs—

still, five years later when everything about you and me had become
complicated and disillusioning and semi-bleak
it was a slight comfort to recall a dream-shot of Wrigley Field
and to say with certainty one thing we could agree on,
one thing not involving any blame or shame, which was
that we were Cubs fans back then, definitely, side by side.

Granted

We received your petition for more life
and here is our response.

Our records indicate that we have given you this response before
but you did not acknowledge receipt.

After thorough study of your situation, we have decided
to grant your request, with the following specification:

You may continue to live for *a while*.
Please be apprised that this disposition of your case
is in fact the most favorable disposition that could have been
hoped for. Lives on earth longer than *a while*
are not possible and therefore cannot be petitioned for.

We note that in fact this disposition was in effect
for a considerable period before you first sent your petition,
so that technically your petition has not resulted in any
alteration of your prospect; but we are familiar with
the kinds of concern that prompt such petitions,
as we have been dealing with them for quite a while.

ANNA O'CONNOR

Day-joy

Give me some plain task: a stack of plates
to soap and dry unwatched. Let me linger
with some purpose in this place. The kitchen
rings with the creakboard step of that
creature I love from the corner of my eye.
What's brightest, if you reach, might bolt;
the sunlight on the floor's unstill, this warmth
is a grazing thing.

Game Theory: A Primer

Moving circles around a campfire the mind is
Anywhere summer sweeps into the room swatting at
Mosquitoes incandescent with the blood of many
Action figures smoking on the back porch of the lakeside
Theatre watching lily pads take over the lagoon
Wide-eyed as a treed raccoon and whether I'm thinking about
Tony's chemo Amber's yard sale Carmen's latest interview
Or the house that wouldn't sell before every floorboard
And shingle was replaced piece by piece until the house
Itself was facsimile or fiction or history repeating
The mind loses glasses umbrellas pens misplaces
Keys homework faces forgets who played the role of Ionesco
Or what it had for dinner that warm December night
In La Spezia in the 90s the same rate as ever moving

Circles around an apple tree the ladder is a piece
Of mind the shed is a piece of mind the alley
A short cut through the neighborhood like-
Mindedness to the drugstore past the drawbridge
To the post office by the pioneer cemetery which takes
For granted the blood of many and fills each plot
With holes so that hole within hole empties
Into gravity a history of spontaneous alleles
The mind like ice dismantling the upper hemisphere
Like sneakers strung over telephone wires
Street code for the rapture or alien abduction or other tricks
The mind can play when no one is looking
Over the shoulder of the mountain moving all its pieces
Into sudden skeins of snow geese startled from the field

ALEX LEMON

Here We Go Volcano

I want to send
All of you good

People out proper
But here I am in

My skivvies, hiding
From the light, still,

Always, speaking to
The dead. The sun goes

Up & so quick it folds
Itself into a valentine

Of blackness. Fireflies
String trotlines of light

In the dusk air. It makes
It easier thinking that

Everyone else is struggling
To do just enough to get

By. All night the lantanas
Endlessly murmur.

Wondering why people
Shout all the time

Is making me dead on
The inside. For the briefest

Moment, each arrangement
Of our bones supports

Singing meat. Then comes
The sagging, the waste—

Then hackberry, the breath
Before the spider bites

That do not stop. I say
Bring the wind mouth to all that.

Heart nail, I shout into
The exploding light—*Forever
Bright in the junkyard.* If they come

To take me away first, swear into
Their eyes that you didn't see shit.

Bios

KELLI RUSSELL AGODON's fourth collection of poems, *Dialogues with Rising Tides*, was published by Copper Canyon Press in 2021. She is the cofounder of *Two Sylvias Press* as well as the Co-Director of Poets on the Coast: A Weekend Retreat for Women. Agodon lives in a sleepy seaside town in Washington State where she is an avid paddleboarder and hiker.

ABDUL ALI is the winner of the 2014 New Issues Poetry Book Prize for his collection, *Trouble Sleeping* (New Issues, 2015). He is from New York but lives in Baltimore. Most recently, Ali received the Ruby fellowship from the Robert Deutsch Foundation for his next poetry project.

HUMBERTO AK'ABAL (1952–2019) was a K'iche' Maya poet from Guatemala. His book *Guardián de la caída de agua* (*Guardian of the Waterfall*) was named book of the year by Association of Guatemalan Journalists and received their Golden Quetzal award in 1993. In 2004 he declined to receive the Guatemala National Prize in Literature because it is named for Miguel Ángel Asturias, whom Ak'abal accused of encouraging racism. The recipient of a Guggenheim fellowship, Ak'abal passed away on January 28th, 2019. For more information, see page 13.

JESÚS AMALIO LUGO is a writer and a biomedical engineer. He has received honorable mentions for the Roberto Bolaño poetry prize (2017), the JL Gabriela Mistral poetry prize (2018), and the Rafael Cadenas poetry prize (2018), and he received second place for the Fernando Santiván story contest (2019). For more information, see page 159.

SOPHIA DE MELLO BREYNER ANDRESEN (1919–2004) is considered one of Portugal's most important 20th century poets. Among her many awards are the Grand Prize for Poetry of the Portuguese Writers Society, the Critics' Prize from the International Association of Critics, the Camões Prize, the Max Jacob Prize, and the Reina Sofia Prize. For more information, see page 83.

EMILY BANKS is the author of *Mother Water* (Lynx House, 2020). Her poems have appeared in *The Cortland Review, Heavy Feather Review, Superstition Review, 32 Poems*, and elsewhere. She lives in Atlanta, where she teaches literature and creative writing as a visiting assistant professor at Emory University.

BROOKE BARRY was raised by bulldogs on a farm in South Georgia. Her memoir-in-progress, *Creatures Like Us*, has received scholarships to the Sewanee Writers' Conference, Writers in Paradise, and Looking Glass Rock Writers' Conference. She has received two Academy of American Poets Awards. Her poetry was shortlisted for the *Montreal International Poetry Prize* and appears in *Columbia Poetry Review*, *The Florida Review*, *New South*, *Salt Hill Journal*, and elsewhere. She lives in Beaufort, South Carolina.

MICHAEL BAZZETT has published four collections of poetry, most recently *The Echo Chamber*, (Milkweed, 2021). A recipient of awards from The Frost Place and the NEA, his poems have appeared in *American Poetry Review*, *The Nation*, *The Sun*, *Tin House*, and elsewhere. His verse translation of the Mayan creation epic, *The Popol Vuh*, (Milkweed, 2018) was named one of 2018's best books of poetry by the *New York Times* and was longlisted for the National Translation Award.

GEOFFREY BROCK has published two poetry collections, most recently *Voices Bright Flags* (Waywiser, 2014). The recipient of a Guggenheim Fellowship, he has translated numerous books from Italian, most recently Giuseppe Ungaretti's *Allegria*, which won the National Translation Award in Poetry. Brock teaches at the University of Arkansas.

DAVID M. BRUNSON's poems and translations appear in *Asymptote*, *The Literary Review*, *Mānoa: A Pacific Journal of International Writing*, *Washington Square Review*, and elsewhere. He is editor and translator of *A Scar Where Goodbyes Are Written: The Poetry of Venezuelan Migrants in Chile*, forthcoming from LSU Press.

SEAN CHO A. is the author of *American Home* (Autumn House, 2021) winner of the Autumn House Publishing chapbook contest. His work can be future found or ignored in *The Massachusetts Review*, *Nashville Review*, *The Penn Review*, *Pleiades*, and elsewhere. He is a PhD student at the University of Cincinnati.

MARTHA COLLINS' eleventh book of poems, *Casualty Reports*, is forthcoming from the University of Pittsburgh in fall 2022. Her most recent book, *Because What Else Could I Do* (2019), won the Poetry Society of America's William Carlos Williams Award. Previous books include *Admit One: An American Scrapbook* (U of Pittsburgh, 2016), *White Papers* (2012), *Blue Front* (Graywolf, 2006), and the paired volumes *Day Unto Day* (2014) and *Night Unto Night* (Milkweed, 2018). Collins founded the UMass-Boston creative writing program and later served as Pauline Delaney Professor of Creative writing at Oberlin College.

KEVIN CRAFT lives in Seattle and directs the Written Arts Program at Everett Community College. His first book, *Solar Prominence* (2005), was selected by Vern Rutsala for the Gorsline Prize from Cloudbank Books. His second collection, *Vagrants & Accidentals* (2017), was published in the Pacific Northwest Poets Series of the University of Washington Press. Editor of *Poetry Northwest* from 2009–2016, he now serves as executive editor of Poetry NW Editions.

BRITTNY RAY CROWELL is a native of Texarkana, Texas. She has received the Donald Barthelme Prize in Poetry and the Lucy Terry Prince Prize, judged by Major Jackson. Her poems appear in *Frontier*, *Glass Poetry*, *The Journal*, *The West Review*, in the anthology *Black Lives Have Always Mattered*, and elsewhere. She is a PhD candidate at the University of Houston.

MADELINE HAZE CURTIS has had fiction featured in *The Forge Literary Magazine* and *West Branch*, among other publications. She is an MFA candidate at the University of Wisconsin–Madison.

MICHAEL DUMANIS is the author of the poetry collections *Creature* (Four Way, 2023; forthcoming) and *My Soviet Union* (UMass, 2007), and co-editor of *Legitimate Dangers: American Poets of the New Century*. New poems appear in *American Poetry Review*, *The Believer*, *Colorado Review*, *The Common*, and elsewhere. He lives in Vermont, teaches at Bennington College, and edits *Bennington Review*.

JAMES ELLENBERGER was born and raised in Chicora, a small town in western Pennsylvania. His work has appeared or is forthcoming in *Beloit Poetry Journal*, *River Teeth*, *Sou'Wester*, *Third Coast*, and elsewhere. He was awarded an Ohio Arts Council Individual Excellence Award in 2020.

CHANDA FELDMAN is the author of *Approaching the Fields* (LSU, 2018). Her recent poems appear in *The Gettysburg Review*, *Poetry*, and *The Southern Review*. She teaches in the creative writing program at Oberlin College.

GARY FINCKE's most recent collections are *The Mussolini Diaries* (Serving House, 2020) and *The Infinity Room* (Michigan State, 2019), which won the Wheelbarrow Books Prize. Collections of his stories and essays have won the Flannery O'Connor Prize and the Robert C. Jones Prize for Short Prose, respectively.

ROBERT LONG FOREMAN's most recent books are *Weird Pig* and *I Am Here to Make Friends*. His work has appeared in *AGNI*, *Crazyhorse*, *Harvard Review*, *Kenyon Review Online*, and elsewhere. He lives in Kansas City, Missouri.

MELISSA GINSBURG is the author of the novels *The House Uptown* and *Sunset City*, the poetry collection *Dear Weather Ghost*, and three poetry chapbooks. A second poetry collection, *Doll Apollo*, will be published by LSU Press in 2022. Her poems appear in *The New Yorker*, *Southwest Review*, *Tupelo Quarterly*, *West Branch*, and elsewhere. She teaches at the University of Mississippi in Oxford.

MATTY LAYNE GLASGOW is the author of *deciduous qween* (Red Hen, 2019), winner of the Benjamin Saltman Award. His poems appear in *Crazyhorse*, *Denver Quarterly*, *Ecotone*, *Gulf Coast*, and elsewhere. He is a Vice Presidential Fellow at the University of Utah where he serves as the Wasatch Writers in the Schools Coordinator and the managing editor of *Quarterly West*.

PAUL GUEST is the author of four collections of poetry, most recently *Because Everything Is Terrible* (Diode, 2018), and a memoir, One More Theory About Happiness (Ecco, 2011). His writing appears in *American Poetry Review*, *The Paris Review*, *Poetry*, *Tin House*, and elsewhere. A Guggenheim Fellow and Whiting Award winner, he lives in Charlottesville, Virginia.

MARK HALLIDAY directs the creative writing program at Ohio University. His seventh book of poems, *Losers Dream On*, appeared in 2018 from the University of Chicago Press. He loves Kenneth Fearing and Stevie Smith.

BRIAN HENRY is the author of eleven books of poetry, most recently *Permanent State* (Threadsuns, 2020). He has translated Tomaž Šalamun's *Woods and Chalices* (Harcourt, 2008), Aleš Debeljak's *Smugglers* (BOA, 2015), and five books by Aleš Šteger. His work has received numerous honors, including two NEA fellowships, the Alice Fay di Castagnola Award, a Howard Foundation fellowship, and the Best Translated Book Award.

NIKI HERD co-edited with Meg Day *Laura Hershey: On the Life & Work of an American Master* (Pleiades Press, 2019). Her poetry, essays, and criticism appear in the *Academy of American Poets Poem-a-Day*, *The Rumpus*, *Salon*, and elsewhere. She is a Visiting Writer in Residence at Washington University in St. Louis.

ROME HERNÁNDEZ MORGAN is a queer Mexican-American writer from Texas. She is currently pursuing a PhD at the University of Cincinnati, where she is a Provost Fellow. Her poetry appears in *Blackbird*, *The Journal*, and *New Ohio Review*.

GRAHAM HILLARD has contributed work to *The Believer, Epoch, Image, Notre Dame Review,* and elsewhere. He teaches at Trevecca Nazarene University in Nashville and is the founding editor of the *Cumberland River Review.*

DAVID KEPLINGER's recent books include *The Long Answer: New & Selected Poems* (Texas A&M UP, 2020) and *Another City* (Milkweed, 2018), which was awarded the 2019 UNT Rilke Prize. In 2020 he won the Emily Dickinson Prize from the Poetry Society of America. His work has appeared in *New England Review, The New Republic, Ploughshares, Poetry,* and elsewhere.

While they've only met once, SOPHIE KLAHR and COREY ZELLER have been writing together since 2012. Klahr is the author of *Meet Me Here at Dawn* (YesYes, 2016). Zeller is the author of *You and Other Pieces* (Civil Coping Mechanisms, 2015) and *Man Vs. Sky* (YesYes, 2013). Their collaborative work appears in *Alaska Quarterly Review, Denver Quarterly, Passages North, The Rumpus,* and elsewhere.

VIRGINIA KONCHAN is the author of four poetry collections, most recently *Bel Canto* (Carnegie Mellon, 2022), *Hallelujah Time* (Véhicule, 2021), and *Any God Will Do* (Carnegie Mellon, 2020), as well as a short-story collection and several chapbooks.

PETER LaBERGE's chapbooks are *Makeshift Cathedral* (YesYes, 2017) and *Hook* (Sibling Rivalry, 2015). His work received a 2020 Pushcart Prize and has appeared in *AGNI, Best New Poets, New England Review, Pleiades,* and elsewhere. He is the founder and editor-in-chief of *The Adroit Journal,* as well as an MFA candidate and Writers in the Public Schools Fellow at New York University.

NICK LANTZ is the author of four collections of poetry, most recently *You, Beast* (U of Wisconsin, 2017). He teaches in the MFA program at Sam Houston State University in Huntsville, Texas.

LANCE LARSEN is the author of five poetry collections, most recently *What the Body Knows* (U of Tampa, 2018). His awards include a Pushcart Prize and fellowships from Sewanee, the Anderson Center and the National Endowment for the Arts. He teaches at Brigham Young University, where he serves as department chair and fools around with aphorisms. In 2017 he completed a five-year appointment as Utah's poet laureate.

ALEX LEMON is the author of five poetry collections and two memoirs, most recently *Another Last Day* Milkweed, 2019) and *Feverland: A Memoir in Shards* (2017). He has received numerous awards including a Fellowship from the NEA and a Jerome Foundation Grant. He lives in Fort Worth, Texas, and teaches at Texas Christian University.

ALEXIS LEVITIN has published 47 books in translation. He has received fellowships from the National Endowment for the Arts, the National Endowment for the Humanities, the Witter Bynner Foundation, and Columbia University's Translation Center, which awarded him the Fernando Pessoa Prize. He has held Fulbright lectureships in Portugal, Brazil, and Ecuador.

ADA LIMÓN is the author of six books of poetry, including *The Carrying* (Milkweed, 2018), which won the National Book Critics Circle Award for Poetry, and *The Hurting Kind*, forthcoming in 2022. She is also the host of the poetry podcast, *The Slowdown*.

CATE LYCURGUS' poetry has appeared or is forthcoming in *Best American Poetry 2020*, *Best New Poets 2019*, *New England Review*, *The Rumpus*, and elsewhere. She has received scholarships from the Bread Loaf and Sewanee Writers' Conferences and was named one of *Narrative*'s 30 Under 30 Featured Writers. She lives south of San Francisco, California, where she interviews for *32 Poems* and teaches professional writing.

MARC McKEE is the author of five collections of poems, most recently *Meta Meta Make-Belief* (Black Lawrence, 2019). His poetry appears in *American Poetry Review*, *Bennington Review*, *Conduit*, *Crazyhorse*, and elsewhere. He is the managing editor of the *Missouri Review* and lives and parents in Columbia, Missouri.

AMY MILLER's writing has appeared in *Barrow Street*, *Gulf Coast*, *Willow Springs*, *ZYZZYVA*, and elsewhere. Her full-length poetry collection *The Trouble with New England Girls* (Concrete Wolf, 2018) won the Louis Award, and her chapbooks include *I Am on a River and Cannot Answer* (BOAAT, 2016) and *Rough House* (White Knuckle, 2016). She lives in Oregon.

KELLY MOFFETT has published several poetry collections and chapbooks, most recently *Just After* (Angels Flight, 2021) and *Dog Year*, forthcoming from Salmon Poetry. She teaches at Northern Kentucky University and is a recent Fulbright Scholar. Her work appears in *The Cincinnati Review*, *Colorado Review*, *Laurel Review*, *Rattle*, and elsewhere.

JENNY MOLBERG is the author of two poetry collections, most recently *Refusal* (LSU, 2020), and LSU will publish her third collection, *The Court of No Record*, in 2023. An NEA Fellow, she has published work in *Gulf Coast*, *The Missouri Review*, *Ploughshares*, *West Branch*, and elsewhere. She teaches at the University of Central Missouri, where she directs Pleiades Press and co-edits *Pleiades* magazine.

ALICIA MOUNTAIN is the author of *High Ground Coward* (Iowa, 2018), winner of the Iowa Poetry Prize, and *Four in Hand* (BOA, forthcoming 2023). She was a Clemens Doctoral Fellow at the University of Denver. She is a lesbian poet based in New York.

JOHN A. NIEVES has recent poems in *Harvard Review*, *The Massachusetts Review*, *North American Review*, *32 Poems*, and elsewhere. He won the Indiana Review Poetry Contest, and his first book, *Curio* (Elixir, 2014), won the Elixir Press Annual Poetry Award Judge's Prize. He teaches at Salisbury University and edits *The Shore Poetry*.

ANNA O'CONNOR is an American writer and visual artist whose poetry, fiction and artwork have appeared in *From Arthur's Seat*, *The Scores*, *Stereoscope Magazine*, and *Windowcat*. She lives in Edinburgh, Scotland.

JOHN POCH's most recent book of poems is *Texases* (WordFarm, 2019). He teaches in the English Department at Texas Tech University.

Originally from New Jersey, MARIA POULATHA has been living in Athens, Greece, with her husband and daughter for the past twenty years. Her short stories have appeared in *Gordon Square Review*, *SmokeLong Quarterly*, and *Split Lip Magazine*.

ALYSSA QUINN is the author of the forthcoming novel *Habilis* (Dzanc, 2022) and the prose chapbook *Dante's Cartography* (The Cupboard Pamphlet, 2019). Her work appears in *Cream City Review*, *Indiana Review*, *Ninth Letter*, *Third Coast*, and elsewhere.

TOMAŽ ŠALAMUN (1941-2014) published more than 55 books of poetry in Slovenia. Translated into over 25 languages, his poetry received numerous awards, including the Jenko Prize, the Prešeren Prize, the European Prize for Poetry, and the Mladost Prize. In the 1990s, he served for several years as the Cultural Attaché for the Slovenian Embassy in New York, and later held visiting professorships at various universities in the U.S. For more information, see page 35.

LIS SANCHEZ has published poetry in *The Cincinnati Review*, *Harvard Review Online*, *Prairie Schooner*, *Spillway*, and elsewhere. She has received a North Carolina Arts Council Writer's Fellowship, *Prairie Schooner*'s Virginia Faulkner Award for Excellence in Writing, *Nimrod*'s Editors' Choice Award, and *The Greensboro Review* Award for Fiction.

Born in Madrid, SANDRA SANTANA is a Spanish poet, critic, translator, and professor. For more information, see page 107.

INDRANI SENGUPTA is a poet from Kolkata, India, currently braving Illinois weather. She received her MFA in poetry from Boise State University. Her work appears in *Colorado Review*, *Hayden's Ferry Review*, *Indiana Review*, *PANK*, and elsewhere.

MATTHEW THORBURN is the author of seven poetry collections, most recently *The Grace of Distance* (LSU, 2019), a finalist for the Paterson Poetry Prize. He has received a Witter Bynner Fellowship from the Library of Congress and fellowships from the Bronx and New Jersey arts councils. He lives with his family in New Jersey.

COREY VAN LANDINGHAM is the author of *Antidote* (Ohio State UP, 2013) and *Love Letter to Who Owns the Heavens*, forthcoming from Tupelo Press. She is a recipient of a National Endowment for the Arts Fellowship and a Wallace Stegner Fellowship from Stanford University, and her poems have appeared in *American Poetry Review*, *Best American Poetry*, *Boston Review*, *The New Yorker*, and elsewhere. She teaches in the MFA program at the University of Illinois.

KATE WEINBERG grew up in Baltimore, Maryland, and lives in Austin, Texas. She earned her MFA in fiction from UC Riverside, her BFA in acting from DePaul University, and also has a background as an improviser, birth doula, comprehensive sex educator, and hospice worker. She was awarded a 2021 grant from the Elizabeth George Foundation and a 2020 fiction fellowship from the Vermont Studio Center.

MARCUS WICKER is the author of two poetry collections, most recently *Silencer* (Houghton Mifflin Harcourt, 2017), which won the Society of Midland Authors Award. He has received a National Endowment for the Arts Fellowship, a Tennessee Arts Fellowship, a Pushcart Prize, a Ruth Lilly Fellowship, and fellowships from the Fine Arts Work Center in Provincetown and Cave Canem. He teaches at the University of Memphis.

CORRIE WILLIAMSON is the author of the poetry collections *The River Where You Forgot My Name* (SIU, 2019), finalist for the 2019 Montana Book Award, and *Sweet Husk* (Perugia, 2014). She was the 2020 recipient of the PEN Northwest/ Boyden Wilderness Writing Residency, spending seven and a half months in a remote, off-grid cabin in Oregon along the wild Rogue River. Recent work appears in *Boulevard*, *Ecotone*, *The Southern Review*, and *Terrain.org*.

TARA ISABEL ZAMBRANO is the author of *Death, Desire and Other Destinations* (2020), a full-length flash collection from OKAY Donkey Press. Her work appears in *CRAFT*, *Post Road*, and elsewhere. She lives in Texas and is the fiction editor for *Waxwing Literary Journal*.

Required Reading

Kim Addonizio, *Now We're Getting Somewhere* (Mark Halliday)

Kaveh Akbar, *Pilgrim Bell* (Peter LaBerge, Kelly Moffett)

Derrick Austin, *Tenderness* (Chanda Feldman)

Blake Bailey, *Philip Roth: The Biography* (Alexis Levitin)

Polina Barskova, *Air Raid*, trans. Valzhyna Mort (David Keplinger)

Joshua Beckman and Tomaž Šalamun, *Tomaž* (Marc McKee)

Claire-Louise Bennett, *Checkout 19* (Anna O'Connor)

Daniel Biegelson, *of being neighbors* (Robert Long Foreman)

Rick Bragg, *The Speckled Beauty: A Dog and His People* (Brooke Barry)

Alberto Breccia and Juan Sasturain, *Perramus: The City and Oblivion*, trans. Erika Mena (David M. Brunson)

Heather Cahoon, *Horsefly Dress* (Corrie Williamson)

Amina Cain, *Indelicacy* (Virginia Konchan)

Rosa Campbell, *Pothos* (Anna O'Connor)

Anne Carson, *Norma Jean Baker of Troy* (Michael Bazzett)

Aaron Caycedo-Kimura, *Ubasute* (Matthew Thorburn)

Victoria Chang, *Another Lost Year* (Ada Limón)

Victoria Chang, *Dear Memory* (Martha Collins)

Victoria Chang, *Obit* (Amy Miller)

Felicia Rose Chavez, *The Anti-Racist Writing Workshop* (Cate Lycurgus)

Te-Ping Chen, *Land of Big Numbers* (Kate Weinberg)

Rohan Chhetri, *Lost, Hurt, or in Transit Beautiful* (brittny ray crowell)

Don Mee Choi, *DMZ Colony* (Niki Herd)

Franny Choi, *Soft Science* (Indrani Sengupta)

Zinzi Clemmons, *What We Lose* (Abdul Ali)

Andrea Cohen, *Everything* (Geoffrey Brock)

Michael Collier, *The Missing Mountain: New and Selected Poems* (Kevin Craft)

Martha Collins, *Because What Else Could I Do* (Kelly Moffett)

CA Conrad, *Amanda Paradise: Resurrect Extinct Vibration* (Brian Henry)

Eduardo Corral, *Guillotine* (Niki Herd)

Cynthia Cruz, *The Melancholia of Class: A Manifesto for the Working Class* (Virginia Konchan)

Kyle Dargan, *Anagnorisis* (Chanda Feldman)

Dalton Day, *Flood-Letting* (Sean Cho A.)

Kendra DeColo, *I Am Not Trying to Hide My Hungers from the World* (Paul Guest)

Jaquira Diaz, *Ordinary Girls* (Tara Isabel Zambrano)

Natalie Diaz, *Postcolonial Love Poem* (Emily Banks)

Alex Dimitrov, *Love and Other Poems* (Paul Guest)

Rita Dove, *Playlist for the Apocalypse* (Peter LaBerge)

Brian Doyle, *One Long River of Song: Notes on Wonder* (Corrie Williamson)

Mark Eisner and Tina Escaja, *Resistencia: Poems of Protest and Revolution* (David M. Brunson)

JJJJJerome Ellis, *The Clearing* (Alicia Mountain)

Julie R. Enszer, Ed. *Sister Love: The Letters of Audre Lorde and Pat Parker 1974–1989* (Alicia Mountain)

Martín Espada, *Vivas to Those Who Have Failed* (Lis Sanchez)

Melissa Febos, *Girlhood* (Melissa Ginsburg, Tara Isabel Zambrano)

Carolyn Forché, *In the Lateness of the World* (Lis Sanchez)

Elizabeth Bales Frank, *Censorettes* (Matthew Thorburn)

Ross Gay, *Be Holding* (Martha Collins, Cate Lycurgus)

Ross Gay, *Catalog of Unabashed Gratitude* (Lance Larsen)

David Graeber and David Wengrow, *The Dawn of Everything: A New History of Humanity* (Kevin Craft)

Carrie Green, *Studies of Familiar Birds* (Matthew Thorburn)

Garth Greenwell, *Cleanness* (Matty Layne Glasgow)

Kimberly Grey, *System for the Future of Feeling* (John A. Nieves)

Maurice Kilwein Guevara, *Autobiography of So-and-So* (Corey Zeller)

Camille Guthrie, *Diamonds* (Michael Dumanis, Virginia Konchan)

Saidiya Hartman, *Wayward Lives, Beautiful Experiments: Intimate Histories of Riotous Black Girls, Troublesome Women, and Queer Radicals* (Alyssa Quinn)

Tony Hoagland, *The Underground Poetry Metro Transportation System for Souls: Essays on the Cultural Life of Poetry* (Mark Halliday)

James Hoch, *The Last Pawnshop in New Jersey* (Michael Bazzett)

Allison Hutchcraft, *Swale* (Gary Fincke)

Chantal James, *None But the Righteous* (brittny ray crowell)

Gayl Jones, *Palmares* (Emily Banks)

Rodney Jones, *Village Prodigies* (Gary Fincke)

Ilya Kaminsky, *Deaf Republic* (Nick Lantz)

Laura Kasischke, *Lightning Falls in Love* (Nick Lantz)

Donika Kelly, *The Renunciations* (Chanda Feldman, Jenny Molberg)

Christopher Kempf, *What Though the Field Be Lost* (Corey Van Landingham)

Kim Hyesoon, *Sorrowtoothpaste Mirrorcream*, trans. Don Mee Choi (Corey Zeller)

Taisia Kitaiskaia, *The Nightgown & Other Poems* (Indrani Sengupta)

Steven Kleinman, *Life Cycle of a Bear* (Martha Collins)

Laura Kolbe, *Little Pharma* (Alicia Mountain)

Danika Stegeman LeMay, *Pilot* (Sean Cho A.)

Michael Levitin, *Generation Occupy* (Alexis Levitin)

Michael Lewis, *The Undoing Project: A Friendship That Changed Our Minds* (Amy Miller)

Paige Lewis, *Space Struck* (Nick Lantz)

Patricia Lockwood, *No One Is Talking About This* (Maria Poulatha)

Silvina López Medin, *That Salt on the Tongue to Say Mangrove*, trans. Jasmine V. Bailey (John Poch)

Lucia LoTempio, *Hot with the Bad Things* (Jenny Molberg)

Claire Luchette, *Agatha of Little Neon* (Madeline Haze Curtis)

Carmen Maria Machado, *In the Dream House* (Madeline Haze Curtis)

Randall Mann, *A Better Life* (Geoffrey Brock)

Nastassja Martin, *In the Eye of the Wild*, trans. Sophie Lewis (Sophie Klahr)

Valerie Martinez, *Count* (Ada Limón)

Adrian Matejka, *Somebody Else Sold the World* (Marc McKee)

William Maxwell, *So Long, See You Tomorrow* (Graham Hillard)

Patrick McGrath, *Asylum* (Graham Hillard)

Kate McIntyre, *Mad Prairie* (Robert Long Foreman)

Jory Mickelson, *Wilderness//Kingdom* (Corrie Williamson)

Brenda Miller, *An Earlier Life* (Lance Larsen)

Mary Miller, *Biloxi* (Brooke Barry)

Poupeh Missaghi, *trans(re)lating house one* (Rome Hernández Morgan)

Jonah Mixon-Webster, *Stereo(TYPE)* (Marcus Wicker)

Dantiel W. Moniz, *Milk Blood Heat* (Madeline Haze Curtis)

Malena Mörling, *Astoria* (Corey Zeller)

Valzhyna Mort, *Music for the Dead and Resurrected* (Michael Dumanis, David Keplinger)

John Murillo, *Kontemporary Amerikan Poetry* (Abdul Ali)

James Nestor, *Breath: The New Science of a Lost Art* (Alex Lemon)

Mark Nowak, *Social Poetics* (Niki Herd)

Kathryn Nuernberger, *The Witch of Eye* (Jenny Molberg)

Kimberly King Parsons, *Black Light* (Tara Isabel Zambrano)

Torrey Peters, *DeTransition Baby* (Matty Layne Glasgow, Kate Weinberg)

Carl Phillips, *Pale Colors in a Tall Field* (Paul Guest)

Catherine Pierce, *Danger Days* (Gary Fincke)

Nicholas Pierce, *In Transit* (John Poch)

Joy Priest, *Horsepower* (brittny ray crowell)

Kevin Prufer, *The Art of Fiction* (John A. Nieves)

Jacques J. Rancourt, *Brocken Spectre* (Corey Van Landingham)

Natasha Rao, *Latitude* (Kelly Moffett)

Srikanth Reddy, *Underworld Lit* (Indrani Sengupta)

Roger Reeves, *Best Barbarian* (Corey Van Landingham)

Molly Reid, *The Rapture Index: A Suburban Bestiary* (James Ellenberger)

Dolores Reyes, *Eartheater*, trans. Julia Sanches (Michael Bazzett)

Bobby C. Rogers, *Paper Anniversary* (Graham Hillard)

Chet'la Sebree, *Field Study* (David Keplinger)

Danielle Sellers, *The Minor Territories* (Amy Miller)

Diane Seuss, *Frank: Sonnets* (Kelli Russell Agodon, Emily Banks, Cate Lycurgus, Marc McKee)

Patrick Shields, *Pinball* (Maria Poulatha)

Leonora Simonovis, *Study of the Raft* (David M. Brunson)

Julietta Singh, *The Breaks* (Brian Henry)

Maggie Smith, *Goldenrod* (Kelli Russell Agodon)

Zadie Smith, *Intimations* (Abdul Ali)

Lisa Russ Spaar, *Madrigalia: New & Selected Poems* (John Poch)

Maureen Stanton, *Body Leaping Backwards: Memoir of a Delinquent Girlhood* (Robert Long Foreman)

Larissa Szporluk, *Virginals* (Melissa Ginsburg)

Olga Tokarczuk, *Flights*, trans. Jennifer Croft (Maria Poulatha)

Vincent Toro, *Tertulia* (Marcus Wicker)

Paul Tran, *All the Flowers Kneeling* (Peter LaBerge)

Walter R. Tschinkel, *Ant Architecture: The Wonder, Beauty, and Science of Underground Nests* (James Ellenberger)

Divya Victor, *Curb* (Rome Hernández Morgan)

Vanessa Angélica Villarreal, *Beast Meridian* (Melissa Ginsburg)

Esmé Weijun Wang, *The Collected Schizophrenias* (Kate Weinberg)

Kary Wayson, *The Slip* (Kevin Craft)

Caki Wilkinson, *The Survival Expo* (Marcus Wicker)

M. L. Williams, *Game* (Brooke Barry)

Phillip B. Williams, *Mutiny* (Michael Dumanis, Ada Limón)

Christian Wiman, *Survival Is a Style* (Geoffrey Brock)

Kathleen Winter, *Cat's Tongue* (John A. Nieves)

Jane Wong, *How to Not Be Afraid of Everything* (Sophie Klahr)

David Woo, *Divine Fire* (Kelli Russell Agodon)

Tobias Wray, *No Doubt I Will Return a Different Man* (Geoffrey Brock)

Dean Young, *Solar Perplexus* (Mark Halliday)

Felicia Zamora, *I Always Carry My Bones* (Brian Henry)

Michelle Zauner, *Crying in H Mart* (Anna O'Connor)

The Copper Nickel Editors' Prizes

(est. 2015)

(Two $500 prizes are awarded to the "most exciting contributions"
to each issue, as determined by a vote of the *Copper Nickel* staff)

Past Winners

fall 2021 (issue 33)

Natalie Tombasco, poetry
Dan Leach, prose

fall 2020 (issue 31&2)

Michael Bazzett, poetry
Matt Donovan, poetry
Aidan Forster, prose
Kathy Fish, prose

spring 2020 (issue 30)

Andrea Cohen, poetry
Maureen Langloss, prose

fall 2019 (issue 29)

Derek Robbins, poetry
Sam Simas, prose

spring 2019 (issue 28)

Catherine Pierce, poetry
Sarah Anne Strickley, prose

fall 2018 (issue 27)

Jenny Boychuk, poetry
Farah Ali, prose

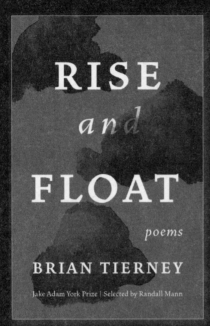

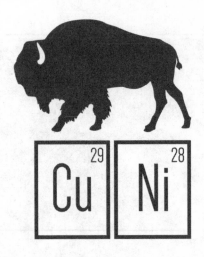

subscription rates

For regular folks:

one year (two issues)—$20
two years (four issues)—$35
five years (ten issues)—$60

For student folks:

one year (two issues)—$15
two years (four issues)—$25
five years (ten issues)—$50

For more information, visit: www.copper-nickel.org

To go directly to subscriptions
visit: coppernickel.submittable.com

To order back issues, email wayne.miller@ucdenver.edu